MW01656855

Remember Me

Remember Me Copyright © 2024 by Inknot Publishing
Published by Inknot Publishing
All rights reserved. Printed in the United States of America. No part of this book may be used or reproduced in any manner whatsoever without written permission except in the case of brief quotations embodied in critical articles or reviews.
This book is a work of fiction. Names, characters, businesses, organizations, places, events, and incidents are either the production of the author's imagination or are used fictitiously. Any resemblance to actual persons, living or dead, events, or locales is entirely coincidental.
Contact info: www.inknotpublishing.com.
Cover Design: Suzanne McCaig
Editors: Kristin McTiernan and Suzanne McCaig
First Edition
ISBN: 979-8-9903605-1-8

For my mom

Thanks for the tea
and memories

Remember Me

Rosemary Toppi

2 Weeks Ago

Chapter One

My daughter Jen accidentally bumped my wheelchair into a cart in the hospital hallway.

"Oops." She and my son Jordan suppressed a laugh.

"Geez, you'd think a nurse would have better wheelchair skills."

"I'm the boss of the nurses. I don't push people anymore. I'm out of practice," she said, stifling a chuckle of laughter.

As we rolled, I said, "I could've walked, you know."

"We know Ma, but we wanted to get there this week," Jordan said.

"Where did you learn such sarcasm?" I joked, knowing full well his attitude came from me.

"I learned from the best." He touched my shoulder. My trembling hand covered his.

In the compact conference room in the cardiology wing, my son and daughter sat on either side of me. Dr. Martinez (my cardiologist), Dr. Brook-Allen (my oncologist), and my assigned medical advocate all sat on the other side of the fake wood table. The French doors made the space seem bigger, but claustrophobia crept up my spine.

It's a full house. Everyone came to tell me I was dying. *As if I didn't know. Do you have to pack me in like a sardine to tell me?*

"Can you open the door, Baby?" My eyes pleaded with my youngest, Jordan, as I reached for my water bottle. He jumped up and popped open the door. The room swirled with fresh air. Well, fresh*er* air.

My kidney cancer that was in remission started growing again last year. Now the one kidney I have left is failing. The medicine to help my kidney tanks my heart. The medicine to help my heart ruins my kidney. At sixty-six years old, I'm not likely to see another birthday.

"Well," Dr. Martinez said. "The best course of action is to keep taking as much Lasix as your kidney will allow and go from there." She turned to Jordan. "She can go home the day after tomorrow." They closed their folders and shook my hand. My kids thanked the doctors as they shook hands.

Why did they thank the doctors? Why aren't they screaming? Jen should have stood with one fist in the air, the other hand grabbing the lapel of Dr. Brook-Allen's superior white coat, saying, "It's 2013, damn it! There must be more you can do!"

Jen and Jordan must be as numb to this run-around as I am. Many times over the last twenty-seven years, Dr. Martinez warned them, "This may be the end. You should say your peace." I suppose they're used to hearing it. It's likely the same as any other day for them. Jordan probably thought, "Oh, ya, okay, Ma's going to die again. Should we get Chinese for lunch?"

"Beth," Dr. Martinez laid her hand on my shoulder and brought her face close to my ear. "You're a fighter. I've seen it through the years. As long as there is life in you, I know you'll take full advantage of it."

Jen bends to hug me in my wheelchair. "We'll all be back in a couple weeks to have an awesome visit. Even Skye is coming."

"Okay, darlin'," I said in my New England accent, so it sounded more like dahlin'. It's my nickname for all my daughters. Three girls: Julie, Jen, and Jess. Calling the girls darlin' helped when I couldn't keep their names straight. My baby boy Jordan didn't come until they were in high school.

"I can't wait to see Sweet Skye. She has been too busy with her new job to visit her Nana."

"Cut her some slack, Ma. She lives in Chicago," Jen said, protective of her daughter.

"Sorry, I know. So do you. I'm glad you came out for this meeting. Thank you. Honestly, though, I can't wait to see everyone," I said as Jordan started rolling my wheelchair out of the conference room.

13 Days Ago

Chapter Two

A few tears rested on the edges of my baby blues as I found myself alone with Dr. Martinez in her office.

"I don't want to be here again," I said.

No stranger to this office, I met Rebecca Martinez when I had my first heart attack. I was thirty-nine then. No matter the season, the aroma of her pine scented candle always wafted from the windowsill.

Three times in the last three months when my pacemaker couldn't keep my heart rhythm steady, my ICD kicked me in the chest, and I called the ambulance. My ICD, an internal defibrillator in my shoulder, just under the skin, has tiny wires that connect tiny paddles to my heart.

"I want the ICD turned off," I said.

Rebecca rose from her chair and sat beside me. "Beth, I need to know if you're sure about this. We have no way of telling how long your heart will work on its own."

The tears that threatened before tumbled down my cheeks and spilled onto my shirt. Dabbing my eyes, I held onto the conviction that brought me here.

"Turn off the machine."

"Your pacemaker will still regulate your heartbeat, but that won't shock you back into rhythm like the ICD does now." She paused and took my hand. "If your heart stops, you will die."

My commitment wavered for a moment, but my mind was made up. I'm going to die soon. I want it to be as peaceful as possible.

I pushed myself up straight in the wheelchair and looked her in the eyes. "I understand."

She nodded. "Would you like me to call Jordan?"

"No, I'm keeping this decision to myself," I said, swallowing back the lump in my throat. "There were too many decisions in my life that were made for me. This one is mine alone."

59 Years Ago

Chapter Three

A sound like stampeding horses thundered up the front porch. I winced as the screen door squeaked, announcing the five-year-old twins, Debbie and Donna, into the kitchen. One girl chased the other around the table, running and shouting as they made fake gun noises.

"Will you guys be quiet?" Patty yelled. She wasn't mad. She had to yell if she wanted to be heard. "Why'd you come in anyway? Take that hullabaloo back outside." She shooed them away with a damp dish towel.

They galloped around the table one more time, pretending their sticks were horses, their dirty tangled hair bouncing behind them. Then the twins scrambled back out the screen door with another creak and bang. This time, they jumped straight off the porch through the broken posts onto the dirt.

I watched it all from my seat at the kitchen table, spooning oatmeal into my almost eight-year-old mouth. Patty braided my long, dark pigtails today. My faded blue dress was getting too short, so my knees showed a little as my legs dangled from my chair, swinging back and forth.

The twins and Patty were only three of my sisters. I had eight. Eight sisters and two brothers. Oldest to youngest went: Sara, Mary, Cathy, Barb, Patty, Tom, me, Mark, Debbie, Donna, and baby Judy. We were all born in this house. Sara, Mary, Cathy, Barb, and Patty had a different dad who died when Patty was three. My three oldest sisters were married with children of their own.

For all the kids my mother, Lizzy Dendin, had, she hardly acknowledged any of us. Almost every year, a new baby was born and handed off to one of my sisters for care. She wasn't here to cook dinner. Patty did that. In fact, Patty cooked all the meals with the little food we had. Lizzy didn't do the laundry; Barb took care of that. Most nights, my mother wasn't home when we went to bed.

My father used to live with us, but he left last year a month after baby Judy was born.

Patty finished the breakfast dishes and got her books ready for school. She looked very neat in her pink dress and black Mary-Jane shoes with folded white socks sticking out at the top. Her hair was in a low ponytail, her bangs straight and severe.

"You'd better wash out that dish before you leave this kitchen," she said right in my face, poking her index finger into my shoulder.

I brandished a false, wide smile. "Yes, your majesty." Her hand struck my face and the sting on my cheek was sharp. "Ow, you didn't have to hit me. I was gonna do it."

Without an apology, Patty left and headed down the road to meet up with her friend Betty. They had been walking to school together ever since I can remember.

My sister, Barb, worked at Charlie's Diner. She was there early this morning, but she would be home with the car soon to take Tom, Mark, and me to school.

Cold water splashed over my hands as I rinsed my bowl in the sink. The sound of tires crushing rocks in the driveway made me think Barb was here. I dried my hands on my skirt and grabbed my schoolbook and slate.

I called out to Tom and Mark, "Come on guys, don't keep Barb waiting! I'll get the twi–." My sentence was cut short as I opened the screen door right onto the uniformed body of a deputy.

There were two of them, accompanied by Miss Harmon, a lovely lady who had been here before. She had on a brown dress with a cream-colored belt and matching gloves. She had candy apple red-framed glasses that turned up at the sides, and brown hair curled just-so under her blue felt hat. Her white heels were already dirty from the driveway.

"Hi honey, remember me? Is your mommy home?" she asked with a practiced smile.

Opening the screen door wide, I let them into the kitchen. "I'll go get her," I said, before I turned and sprinted through the kitchen and up the stairs, passing Tom and Mark on their way to the kitchen.

What I meant by "get her" was "find her". I wasn't sure she was home. As usual, I hadn't seen her yet this morning.

"Ma! Ma! That lady is here again, and she brought deputies," I called from the top of the stairs.

My mother came out of the bathroom cradling her head in one hand and holding her yellow housecoat closed with the other. She had on slippers that used to be yellow but were now a tattered, dirty mess. Her mouth opened to yell at me for being too loud when what I said registered.

Her eyes widened, and she popped back inside the bathroom. Toiletries rattled and the cabinet door slammed. When the bathroom door opened again, she was wearing her nice blue dress with a bright white belt and her hair was combed back into a bun.

She steadied herself on the railing and rubbed her neck as she walked down the stairs. At the bottom of the stairs, I tried to hold her hand. She slipped from my grasp and walked down the short hall.

The two deputies stood near the kitchen sink. Miss Harmon sat at the table with Tom and Mark. I noticed Debbie and Donna's eyes peeking in at the kitchen window.

"Good morning, Lizzy. Please sit down," Miss Harmon said.

As Miss Harmon talked, I realized what was going on, and why the deputies were there. Miss Harmon slid papers across the table. My mother took the pen in her hand and turned to Tom and me with no tears and no words. My eyes couldn't get any bigger. I wanted to look at Tom, but I couldn't take my eyes off my mother. She turned away and signed the papers.

Crickets trapped under the porch chirped louder in the moment's quietness. The clock in the hall ticked and tocked at the last moments of my family. Even though it was a cool morning, sweat beaded on my forehead and above my lip.

Finally, words came bubbling over from somewhere inside me. "Wait a minute!" burst out of my mouth. "What are you doing? What is happening here?" Yelling every word, I continued, "Are you letting them take us away? Do Barb and Patty know about this? What will they say when they come home, and we're gone? Barb will be here to take us to school soon. What will you tell her?"

My mother said nothing to us. She rose from the table, turned her back to us, and walked into the hall.

I started after her. "Ma, please!"

Deputy Larson caught my arm. "Oh no ya don't."

"I don't want to go. Please stop this," I called out to her as she left the room, "Why can't *you* go? You're hardly here anyway."

My mother paused for half a second before she climbed the stairs. She never looked back.

The deputy dragged me out of my house, across the porch, and down the broken stairs. He plopped me into the squad car and held me there with both his hands around my waist.

"Listen you little shit," he said, his nose touching mine, "Don't make me take out my friend here." Letting go of my waist, he patted the wooden club at his side and used the other hand to shut the car door.

I pulled my feet into the car just as the door slammed shut. Rising onto my knees, I pounded on the glass, calling to her.

Miss Harmon came out with baby Judy on her hip. She gave Donna and Debbie each a lollipop and the twins followed her.

Tom, Mark, and Judy went with Miss Harmon in Deputy Wood's vehicle. The twins were placed in Deputy Larson's car with me. The twins looked at me with screwed-up faces. They couldn't understand why I was crying. They had lollies and got to ride in a car. For them, it was a great day.

We drove to the stop sign at the end of our road as Barb's car rounded the corner beside us. The twins waved and smiled at her, but I banged on the window and yelled for help. She went by, watching us with an open mouth. She must have known. She must have known because she just drove on.

We were in the car for what seemed like hours, coming to a large red brick building in a compound of buildings. I was once again wrestled out of the car by deputy Larson as I flailed.

Inside, I learned this building was for eight to eighteen-year-old girls. Two days later, I spent my eighth birthday without my family in the dormitory of a rundown orphanage. I cried into my very small, very flat pillow. I cried for my brothers, the twins, and sweet baby Judy. I cried for myself, too. I had no idea what had become of any of them. Would we grow up apart? Could something like this be temporary? Our home was crazy most days, but at least we were together. Eventually, the room faded into darkness.

The two women who ran the orphanage were always referred to as "The Ladies" when the children were talking about them. They were both salt-and-pepper-haired old spinsters. One was tall and haggard with a low gray bun, and the other was chunky with pink skin and a bobbed haircut. My mouth and attitude afforded me many hours of their punishments in my time at *the* home. *The* home, not my home.

In the first few days, I saw Tom and Mark across the street in a home for boys. The only cafeteria was in their building. The day I saw them, I ran to them. We hugged until The Ladies pulled us apart. They rapped us on the knuckles with a ruler right there while the others ate.

After that day, my stomach would be in knots until I caught their eyes in the breakfast crowd.

56 Years Ago

Chapter Four

A canvas bag was thrust at me. "Your aunt and uncle are here to adopt you. Pack your things and come downstairs."

I placed the clothes from my only drawer into the sack as memories of the past three years flashed through my mind. Now, at eleven years old, my time here was a blur of school, punishment, bullying, and being bullied.

At the bottom of the stairs, I paused. I assumed my Aunt Joan was adopting me. She was the only aunt I knew. I didn't recognize the people standing with the Ladies in the hall. The woman looked young, and she wore pants. I *dreamed* of wearing pants. Before I saw a photo of Amelia Earhart standing in front of her plane, I didn't even know women could wear them. This woman wore glorious green pants with thin black lines that made a checkered design. Her black wool coat was open, and I saw the green flowing fabric of her blouse tied in a big floppy bow around her neck.

The man standing next to her was head and shoulders above her. He had on a dark suit with a thin tie, and his hat was just a bit crooked.

"This is John and Millie Shelby," one of The Ladies said.

Millie's dark hair fell over her shoulders as she bent down and touched her cheek to mine. She made a smooch sound next to my cheek, careful not to get any of her bright red lipstick on my skin.

Over her shoulder, just beyond the big glass doors, Tom stood outside on the concrete. He saw me through the glass and smiled with one hand stuck in the pocket of his jeans, and the other holding onto a young girl.

"Is that baby Judy?" I asked, even though the girl outside was no longer a baby.

Millie nodded, and I ran out to hug them both. "I missed you guys so much,"

"Who are you?" Judy asked.

"I'm your sister, Beth."

"Oh," she said, nodding her head and looking at the ground.

Sitting in the back seat of John and Millie's car with Tom and Judy, curiosity overwhelmed me. "The Ladies said you were our aunt. Did Lizzy tell you where we were?"

Millie turned with her red lips, frowning at the thought of our biological mother. "No. The state called us a few months ago to tell us you were here. I'm your father's sister."

"Oh. How long have you been married?"

Smiling now, Millie touched John's shoulder. "Three years."

"How old are you?" I asked.

"Elizabeth!" Millie snorted with laughter. "You shouldn't ask a lady how old she is. But since we are family, I'll tell you. I'm twenty-three years old."

"Enough questions for now," John said over his shoulder.

After a while, Millie called to the back seat. "We're almost home."

We came to a neighborhood of single-family homes and duplexes with small, gated yards. The driveway we pulled into belonged to a powder blue duplex.

Three kids popped open one of the two screen doors on the porch. I instantly recognized them. Mark, Debbie, and Donna.

"What?" I ran up the concrete steps and grabbed Debbie and Donna in a hug. Mark blazed past me into Tom's arms.

"Quiet now!" I spun around to see who it was. It was a carbon copy of Millie.

Millie came up behind me and said, "This is my twin sister, Jillie. She and her husband Sam have adopted your brother and sisters. They live downstairs and we live above."

"Yes," Jillie said. "And now they're your cousins."

Jillie stood holding the door open. She waved her kids back into the house. Her arm movements were jerky and awkward compared with Millie's. Her thinner face produced harder features as well. Even though there were definite similarities, it wouldn't be hard to tell them apart.

Upstairs, we left our shoes at the door, and Millie showed us around. The apartment was average for a 1950s family. The living room had a floor-unit television with a small square radio on top. There was a flower-spotted couch, a matching loveseat, and chair. Nothing was special about the kitchen except the yellow color of the appliances. Millie walked us down the hall to the bedrooms.

Millie and John's bedroom was first in the hall, then Judy's, with a bathroom on the opposite wall. Judy ran into her room and bounced on her bed. Tom's and my bedroom were next.

"These are your rooms." Millie said with a smile. "I decorated a little but let me know if you want to change anything." She opened both doors. "When the door is closed, I promise John and I will knock before we come in."

In all my eleven years, I had no privacy, never even a thought of it. At Lizzy's, we not only all slept in one room, but we also all slept in the same bed. At the orphanage, there were eleven other beds in the dormitory.

My own space? The hairs prickled on my neck and goosebumps traveled down my arms.

Trying to hide my delight, I asked, "May I go in?"

"Of course."

I closed the door behind me. The metal latch sounded, clicking into place. I was alone. I leaned against the door with my eyes closed and drank in the hush of my own space. I took off my socks and squished my feet into the plush rug that covered the dark hardwood floor.

The room was big enough for my single bed, a tall dresser, and a vanity desk, but not much else. Pink ruffled pillows and a matching blanket covered the bed. On the vanity, there was a shiny brush and comb set and a small pink box. I cradled the box in my hands and lifted the top. A little ballerina popped up and started to twirl. Music twinkled from the small wind-up barrel. Holding the box close, the plinking of the notes tapped my chest. I sat on the floor and leaned my back against the bed and didn't move until I was called to dinner.

The three years at the orphanage did considerable damage to our spirits. The three of us made life miserable for John and Millie. One or all of us acted out regularly.

Tom was at prime hormone age and the testosterone in the air was like a dark cloud. Tom was trying to find something in his life that was his. John was trying to assert his leadership as the father of this new family. A lot of dinners ended with shouting and slamming doors. Sometimes, Tom would storm out of the house and not come back for many hours.

Judy was a terror. She was almost five and always screaming or throwing things. Judy had many spankings and bars of soap wash her mouth out in those first few months.

Being eleven years old, I had imbedded demons of my own. Milly tried her best with an almost endless kindness. There were days when I found myself shouting and starting fights over meaningless things. No matter what started the fights, they always ended the same. I would push way too far, and Millie would slap my face. I would yell something horrible and run to my room.

Chapter Five

There were only a few days of living with "Mom and Dad" and our "cousins" before we were made to attend the local school.

The very first morning, I met Sarah Jane. Her brown hair was longer than mine and bounced around loosely past her shoulders. She walked right up to me and asked, "Are you new?"

I tried to smooth my schedule on one of my books. "Yes. I guess I look pretty lost," I said. The winter sun was reflecting off the snowbanks, making me shade my squinting eyes.

"Kinda." A smile broke out on both of our faces. She looked at my schedule and helped me to my first class. The tan hallways were decorated for Valentine's Day. I gripped my books tight in front of me like a shield as we passed the other kids. My saddle shoes tapped in rhythm with hers on the hard linoleum as she led me to my classroom.

"Look for me at lunch," she said and skipped off to her first class.

At lunch, Sarah Jane stood at her table and waved me over. She introduced Laura, Joe, and Joanie around the table. Joe and Joanie were cousins.

Laura's older brother, Matt, was in high school. After that moment, we would gather and talk every day.

After half a school year and summer with Millie and John, my friends and I entered sixth grade. My home life was mostly turmoil. About once a month, I would skip school and not go home. Sometimes I would tell my friends what I was up to, sometimes I wouldn't. When I didn't come home, John, Millie, and Judy would all pile into the car and drive all over town looking for me.

The last time I attempted this, it was ten at night before they found me. I was down by the train tracks with a cigarette in my hand. John got out of the car and stood in front of me.

"Get. In." he said.

I knew he was looking down at me, but I didn't dare look up. I turned and headed for the car.

"Drive them home. I need a walk," he said. Millie slid over and took the driver's seat without hesitation.

Silent most of the way, Millie drove while I brooded. She turned onto our street, still looking at the road she said, "I really have done the best I could for you. I don't know what will happen tomorrow. Please know that I love you."

"What does that mean? What's so special about tomorrow?"

"Your father will talk with you," she said as she parked in the driveway. Millie left me there while she helped Judy out of the backseat.

The words paralyzed me. My mind raced with possibilities, none of them good.

"Beth, come up and get ready for bed," Millie called from the porch as she opened the screen door and went upstairs.

In a daze, I walked up to the apartment and went through my bedtime routine. I got into bed but struggled to get to sleep.

Late into the night, Millie waited for John in the living room. Her knitting needles clicked in the quiet. We both heard him come in the door downstairs. Once John was in the living room, there were hushed but agitated words I couldn't make out. They talked for a long time, moving from the living room to the kitchen, and finally to their bedroom. They shut their bedroom door, and I was able to nod off as I stared at my ceiling.

No one said a word as we ate breakfast the next morning. Toast kept getting caught in my throat. I drank my orange juice in big gulps to get it down.

As I finished my scrambled eggs, John finally spoke. "If you ever do that again, you are going back to the orphanage."

He was looking right at me. *Could they do that?* My eyes darted to Millie for help. She was looking into her lap, wringing her cloth napkin in her hands.

"Do you understand?" His question jolted me back to his eyes.

Millie's words from yesterday came back to me. She loved me. She had said the words before, but they were like any other words to me before now. They weren't taking me back because she wanted me here. Maybe John did too. I looked back at him and nodded. From that moment, they really were Mom and Dad to me.

Chapter Six

As hard as it was at home, being with my friends was a different world. With my group, it was light and fun. I didn't tell them much about my younger years, but I suspected they knew most of it somehow.

We laughed and shrieked when juicy gossip was shared. Most days, we had to be told to quiet down by one teacher or another. I was also no stranger to the principal's office or detention.

Regularly, after school, we would steal some liquor from Sarah Jane's parents' liquor cabinet. Her parents had lots of parties and never noticed if one or another of the bottles was lower than before. One of us would keep watch for Mrs. Dunbar and another one of us would grab what looked good. One day I grabbed Gin–it tasted like window cleaner. We drank it all the same.

We would steal cigarettes from Joanie's mom. They were always on the counter. If she noticed them going missing, she never said. At the park, under the big willow, we tried to look our coolest as we sucked in the horrible tasting smoke.

I caught the attention of many schoolboys and was the biggest tease. I would wink or blow kisses to all of them. I had crushes on lots of boys, including

Joe. On one of our tipsy days at Sarah Jane's, I got up my nerve. Sitting on the couch in the den, I turned to him and put my head on his shoulder. "Which girl at school do you have a crush on?"

"I don't have a crush on any girl." He took a swig of the current bottle and handed it to me. "I'll be right back." He hopped off the sofa and walked towards the kitchen. That's all I remember. I passed out.

54 Years Ago

Chapter Seven

Strep throat was still a big deal when I was young. Mom kept me shut up in my room with a steady diet of aspirin and penicillin. I whiled away the hours reading magazines, listening to the radio, and having dance parties of one.

On Saturday, the doorbell rang. I tiptoed down the hall as mom went down the stairs. My eyes lit up. It was Laura and Joanie. I wasn't very sick anymore, but Mom wouldn't let them in. My smile fell to a frown. I made it back to my room before anyone caught me.

A moment later there was a thud on my window. I pulled aside the curtain as a snowball exploded against the glass. As it slid down, I saw Laura and Joanie. They stood there bobbing and shivering up to their shins in the January snow.

After some quick gossip, Joanie said, "We wanted to make sure you were okay. We have to go thaw our toes now."

"We're glad you're feeling better. Hope to see you Monday," Laura called over her shoulder as they walked back to the snow-free sidewalk.

After shutting my window, I flopped down onto my bed, staring starry-eyed at the ceiling. *People trudged through the snow to make sure I was okay.*

No friend made me feel important before. At the orphanage, you were grateful if you made it to bed each night alive and unmolested. No one was concerned with anyone else.

Two weeks after Joanie and Laura came to my window, I was sick again. This time with a trip to the hospital. "Rheumatic Fever." Dr. Stricklen told us. My mother gasped, putting her hand on her chest.

Cold sweat dampened my patient gown, and my long dark hair stuck to my face. My head lay heavy on the paper-thin hospital pillow. My shoulders, knees, and back ached as though I aged seventy years overnight.

My third night at the hospital, I had what I now know was a panic attack.

It felt as if my spacious room was getting smaller by the second. The walls seemed as close as they did in "the closet," a punishment favored by The Ladies at the orphanage. They rolled our bed—child and all—into the dormitory closet. The fit was perfect and made me wonder if the closet was built for this purpose. You'd have to stay there hot and hungry until released.

In my hospital bed, I tried to lift my arms to push back the walls. My limbs wouldn't obey. The beating in my chest made my fingers and toes numb. My whole body was wet, and my breath was short. I tried to call the nurse, but only called out above a whisper's volume. I shut my eyes and filled my lungs with as much air as possible.

On my exhalation, the loudest scream my vocal cords would allow escaped my mouth. I screamed as I ripped off my blanket and ran for the door. I screamed when I ran past the nurse in the hallway. I was still screaming when she and two other floor nurses wrestled me to the ground.

Someone slapped me hard in the face. Shocked back from wherever my mind went, I realized I was out of my room and in the light.

I still couldn't breathe, only now it was because a nurse was on my chest. Her hands were heavy on my shoulders. With an eyebrow raised, she asked, "You done?"

I nodded my head, and she climbed off. "Sorry," I said to them all.

The nurse at my feet was unfazed, like this happened every day. She let go of my legs and walked back to her station without acknowledging my apology. I sat on the floor with my head in my hand, my heart still pounding in my chest.

A nurse walked me carefully back to my bed. Each step on the cold, flat tile sent lightning shocks to my heart. She changed the sheets while I changed my gown, both of which had been soaked with sweat. Now climbing into the bed was a comfort. The paper-thin pillow seemed more like a cloud.

"Can you leave the door open?" I asked in a shaky voice.

"Just a crack," she said and left without another word. I dozed off soon after.

The next afternoon, I was released. I never knew if it was because of the midnight episode or because I was well enough to go home. Either way, I was thankful to be in my own bed again, even if I was again confined to my room.

Chapter Eight

Luke moved onto our street–four houses down. He was in the same grade as my brother Tom, but a year older and a bit taller. He had dark hair and light brown eyes, almost golden with flecks of chocolate. Luke became a fixture at our house, and Tom at his. Dad put a net on the side of the garage. The boys had endless practices, so they would be in top form for the high school basketball team.

One day in August, Tom and Luke came into the kitchen after a morning of free throws. Tom tapped the top of my head, and I rolled my eyes.

"Beth," he said on his way down the hall. "Could you get us some lemonade? I'll be back in a minute."

"Your wish is my command." I closed the Ladies' Home Journal, rose from the table, and dipped into a low bow. I gave Luke a wink when I flipped up. My loose brunette hair fell below my shoulders onto my white button-down short-sleeve shirt. I was wearing a full blue skirt and fuzzy slippers.

Luke leaned against the counter. He wiped the sweat off his face with the edge of his t-shirt. I sensed his eyes following me. I put the glasses down on the counter and dared a sideways glance.

When I caught his eye, he smiled and looked away. The already warm kitchen went up ten degrees. I took out the lemonade, poured it, and replaced the pitcher, all without daring another peek.

Handing Luke a glass, I leaned against the counter next to him. His sweaty teen scent filled my head. Heat radiated from him.

He shifted himself right in front of me and I froze. He touched my arm before he leaned down and kissed my cheek, just to the left of my lips. My eyes went wide and when I blinked, he was gone. He grabbed Tom's drink and disappeared down the hallway.

My legs turned to jelly, melting me to the floor with my back against the cabinet. I was still sitting there holding my cheek when my mom came upstairs with her clean laundry basket.

"Why are you on the floor? Did you fall?" she asked, her brow furrowed with concern.

"It's just cooler down here," I lied. "Can I go to Sarah Jane's?"

"Yes, just be back by dinner."

"Thanks." I ran out the door and down the stairs.

Sarah Jane lived five blocks down and around the corner. With no idea if she was home, I turned in her direction. Soon, I found myself sitting on a bench at a small park, still a couple of blocks from Sarah Jane's. Coming to my senses, I laughed out loud at what had just happened.

This boy was different. I had a crush on Luke from the moment I saw him, but he was going to be in High School. I never thought he might be interested in me. Maybe he wasn't, maybe he was just bored and wanted to joke with me. Not funny. That is what I convinced myself. He was just a mean boy playing pranks on his bud's little sister. *Jerk.*

Taking my hair in my fists, trying to put the memory out of my mind, I looked down at the grass. I was looking down at my slippers. Fleeing the scene, I didn't even think about what shoes I had on. I decided not to tell anyone about Luke or the slippers.

51 Years ago

Chapter Nine

Christmas!

Here with these people we now call Mom and Dad, we had a plastic tree. John always put it together and all five of us would decorate it. There were cookies, playful banter, and no arguments for that one day.

The Christmas I was sixteen, we had just finished decorating the tree when Luke knocked on the door. Dad called out for him to come in.

"Hey Luke, what do you think?" Tom called from behind the tree as he hung the last ornament.

"Wow guys, it looks great!" Luke replied.

He stood there, something off in his stance. His face was red, but not from the cold. Had he been crying?

"Are you okay?" I asked Luke. Everyone's attention turned toward him.

"Well, sorry guys, I didn't know I was coming in on your tree decorating, but I got some bad news today. My dad has lung cancer." This tall, sporty young man changed into a vulnerable, trembling teen. "They say they don't even know how long he will live." He wasn't crying, but there were tears in his eyes. He sat on the couch, his head in his hands.

Immediately, Mom was next to him with her arm around him. I stood there silently by the tree.

"Sorry son," Dad managed, standing there with his hand on Luke's shoulder.

"Come to my room," Tom said, and Luke rose. Luke was looking straight at me. I couldn't move or speak. It seemed like he wanted to say something, but he turned and followed Tom.

"I'm going to make the Marcomes a casserole. Maybe a cake too," Mom said as she stood and smoothed her skirt. "We can bring it over to them later. Beth, come help me?" Shaking off the shock, I walked into the kitchen behind her.

Dad stayed in the living room looking at the tree. Soon after, the radio came on and I knew he had settled down in his chair.

I assisted Mom in chopping and slicing. I was pouring the milk into the cake batter when a thought came to me. *What if Luke's father dies and Luke needs to move?* I found tears in my eyes for Tom losing someone else in his life. I would miss Luke too. My heart was breaking for us all.

My mother interrupted my thoughts, "In times like these, it is important to help as much as possible. Anything we can do for the Marcome's frees up more time for them to be together as a family."

I threw myself into her statement. For the next two months, I would be a daily fixture at the Marcome household. I took on as many of Mrs. Marcome's daily responsibilities as she would allow.

Just before Valentine's Day, Luke's father went into the hospital. Four days later, Mr. Marcome passed away with his wife, his sister, and Luke by his side.

A few days after the funeral, Luke rang our doorbell.

"Tom's at work," I said.

"Actually, I was hoping *you* had a minute."

Sitting across from each other, we leaned on the wrought iron porch banisters. I fiddled with my nails and stole peeks at him out of the corner of my eye. He stared at the concrete steps.

"Tom wouldn't like this if he knew," he started. "But I've felt a connection to you from the first time

I saw you." Luke turned to me with a half-smile. "You were out on the porch with your cousin Debbie. I was driving by with my mother and saw you sitting there. I was so happy to find out you had a brother my age. I could see you all the time."

He scooted over, took my hand, and went on, "I love hanging out with Tom. He's my best friend, but every day I hoped to see you and was so happy when you were there."

My mouth hung wide open. I said, "When you kissed me years ago, I decided it was a joke. It was the quickest peck on the cheek, and you said nothing about it. I was mad at you for so long." My eyes turned to the ground.

Luke continued to talk quietly. "I tried not to like you. I dated other girls, but I couldn't stop thinking of you and hoping someday you would like me. You and your family have been so good to us. Especially in these past months with my dad's cancer. My feelings for you have grown, and I had to tell you."

I didn't dare move.

"I want you to be my girlfriend, Beth. Go steady with me. I'll tell Tom," Luke declared.

It was so sudden, but I knew I cared for him too. *My parents would have a conniption.*

"Luke, I want to date you too, but I can't go steady. I'm only sixteen."

"Then it will be our secret for now. If you will have me, I want to be your boyfriend." He was whispering now, as if we were planning a bank robbery.

"Yes." I whispered back, and he kissed me on my cheek–not so secretly–on my front porch.

We were hardly ever alone together, only in stolen moments. There were secret smiles when no one was looking and quick kisses when no one was around.

Luke got a job at the hardware store and sometimes I would go there, pretending my dad needed something. Luke would have to show me where the item was, of course, and we would steal a moment in the aisles.

Sometimes there was a detour to the supply closet if no one was looking. Those were moments we cherished. Still rushed, still secret, but all ours. We kissed without looking out of the corner of our eyes. Deep, long, not nearly satisfying enough kisses that tasted of penny candy with roaming hands and mussed hair.

Luke finished 11th grade, and I finished my sophomore year. One summer day, we planned a getaway together.

"Sarah Jane, I need a big favor!" I begged when I called her Friday morning. "I need to tell my mom

I'm spending the day with you tomorrow. Will you cover for me if she asks?"

"Sure, if you tell me what you'll really be doing." I could hear Sarah Jane's smile in her voice.

"I'll tell you later, I promise."

That night at dinner, "Can Sarah Jane and I spend the day at the pool tomorrow?" I asked Mom. Dad drove delivery trucks and was out on a run at the time, thank heaven.

"Of course, it should be a hot one. It'll be nice to cool off there. Judy and I are going to the Johnson's for a birthday party, or we may have joined you." Bullet dodged. I didn't even think of that possibility.

In the morning, I scarfed my breakfast and changed for a day at the pool.

"Bye, have a nice day," Mom called from the living room. "Do you want some sandwiches for lunch?"

"No, thank you. Sarah Jane's mom is making some." I called back over my shoulder, trying to sound as natural as possible. "See you later. Have a good time at the Johnson's." A sigh of relief washed over me, knowing that Mom would not be seeing Sarah Jane's mom today. Mrs. Dunbar was visiting her mother with Sarah Jane's younger brother, and she wouldn't be home until Sunday afternoon.

I went down the road toward Sarah Jane's house but stopped at a small park. Luke waited there. We walked to his car hand in hand. I slid onto the bench seat when he opened my door. Luke jumped through the driver's window.

"I thought we could go to Eaton. There's a park there and no one from town should be there," he said with his gorgeous smile.

"Sounds good to me." I slid to the middle of the blue vinyl seat to hug his arm.

We spent most of the ride quietly, just listening to the radio. I had my head on his shoulder and the biggest smile on my face. Eaton was about an hour and a half away, and as we drove, I dozed off. I woke up when my head hit the dashboard.

Chapter Ten

"Are you alright?" Luke asked from somewhere that sounded far away.

Dazed in shock and pain, I forgot where I was. Just as I remembered, there was another slam. It threw me into the passenger side door. A shooting pain went up my right arm, then darkness.

I woke up to someone taking me from the car and laying me on what seemed to be a bed. I'd forgotten what was going on again.

They must have seen my eyes open because now there was a man in my face. He asked, too loudly, "Can you tell me your name? Honey, do you know your name?"

After wondering a moment if I *did* know my name, I said, "Beth, my name is Elizabeth Shelby." Trying to sit up, things got dazzling bright and then dark.

When my eyes opened again, I saw a plain white ceiling. This time, I knew right away that it was a hospital room. Mom was sitting on a red chair in the corner reading a magazine. Judy was looking out the window. She wore a pretty, pink dress covered with tiny white flowers. She reminded me of our sister Patty.

It smelled like disinfectant. The light from the window pierced my eyes and seemed to go straight into my brain. I tried to raise my hand to shield my eyes and realized it was in a cast and pinned to my chest.

"Ow!" My outburst made them look at me. Mom rushed to the bed and stroked my hair.

"Your arm is broken," she said, looking into my eyes. "And you have a concussion."

"Where is Luke? Is he okay? What even happened?" I tried to sit up a little more in bed.

"Your brother brought him home," Mom said. "Luke has bruised ribs and some cuts and bruises." She helped me adjust, then fluffed the pillows.

Why was Mom being so nice? She must know I lied by now.

"How long have I been here? Where are we, anyway?"

"We just got here. They called us when you came in about an hour ago," she said. "This is Union Hospital. To say we were surprised to get the call is an understatement. *I* thought you were at the pool." *There it is.* Mom's eyebrows raised in that way that moms' eyebrows do when they know they caught you in a lie. "We were just about to leave for the Johnson's."

I looked out the window, then back to Mom. "I'm sorry I lied. Luke and I have been dating in secret since his dad died in February." I looked back and forth between Judy and Mom. "What happened to us, anyway?"

"The police officer told me you and Luke were hit from the side by someone who ran a stop sign. The driver didn't see Luke stop for the boy on the bike."

"I dozed off. I never saw the boy or the person who hit us," I said. "I woke up when my head hit the dashboard." I raised my left hand to touch my forehead. "Can I go home?" As I asked, the doctor opened the door and walked in. Dad strode in right behind the doctor. My heart skipped when our eyes met. He was supposed to be gone until tomorrow morning.

"You are one lucky young lady," the doctor said as he looked at my chart. "You can go home in just a little while, but you must stay in bed." My eyes weren't on him, they were on Dad.

"Oh, she will stay in bed alright," Dad said, looking straight at me. I knew he knew, and that wasn't good.

"I'd like to go home. I'll take it easy," I said. The doctor nodded and left the room to fill out the papers.

My dad sat forward on the red chair with his elbow on his knees, one balled-up fist under his chin. A position all the family knew well. It was how he sat just before we got lectured or punished.

The lecture never came. After a minute, that seemed like an hour, he got up and walked out of the room. Mom and I looked at each other. "Let me go talk to him," she said and walked out the door.

"He got home early just before the hospital called. Boy, you made him madder than I have ever seen," Judy giggled after Mom left. "He probably thinks you were running away again."

"This wasn't like that." I raised my good hand to cover my mouth. "I promised I would never do that again."

Had he really thought I was running away? It had been about four years since breakfast when he told me he would send me back to the orphanage. *I'm almost seventeen now. Could they even take me back?*

When Dad reentered the room, the man who had truly become my father, I launched into a flutter of speech. "I wasn't running away. It was just a fun trip. Sorry I lied. Please, please don't send me back," Tears started streaming from my eyes, "to the orphanage."

Turning to my good side, I stuffed my face into the pillow. Mom came to the bedside and stroked my hair.

"Oh sweetie, we wouldn't do that. We never thought that was happening."

"As soon as I saw Dad and how upset you both were, it reminded me of when I was younger. This wasn't like that," I said, with my face still stuffed in the pillow.

Now Dad was at my side with his hand on my shoulder and dampness in his eyes. "I'm sorry I ever said that. I was at my wit's end then. I know this was different. You've been so good since then, I forgot all about it. We'll never make you go back there again."

I looked at Judy, and she was crying, too. It was rare to see her cry. Harshness was ingrained in her. In some ways, she had it hardest. In her toddler years, when a person is supposed to have the most love and attention, she was just ignored and abandoned. I reached out and hugged her as tightly as I could with my good arm.

We all just sat there close and quiet for a few minutes, then Dad spoke. "The doctor said we can go home Let's get some ice cream on the way?" We all brightened at this; it was a great family treat to get ice cream.

Chapter Eleven

I had a full week of bed rest. The long wooden cooking spoon digging into the itchy depths of my cast was the only relief. My friends randomly stopped in. Their tanned skin and sticky pool hair tormented me in my overheated room. Everyone had come except the one person I wanted to see, Luke. He had not even come over to talk to Tom.

The day I could finally eat breakfast at the kitchen table, Dad was on a shipping run. As I finished breakfast, I asked, "Why hasn't Luke come by? Has Tom said anything?"

Mom froze at the sink. "He came by the very first day you were home. You were asleep and your dad talked with him in the living room," she said without turning around. "There were hushed voices, but I did manage to hear your father tell Luke he was disappointed in him for keeping secrets. He thought it was best if Luke stayed away for a little while."

"What?" I said louder than I meant to. Mom jumped and a soapy bowl slipped from her gloved hands. It crashed but didn't break in the sink. "Why didn't you tell me this before?"

"I'm sorry, honey." She half turned to me. "It was a choice we made. We love Luke, but we think you are too young to be so serious with someone."

Staring at the last four Cheerios floating in my bowl, I boiled inside. I stood, walked into my room, and closed the door.

I pulled my hair into a high ponytail and put on sandals, then walked down the stairs and right out the front door. "Beth!" I heard my mother call me, but I didn't turn back. I proceeded up the street toward Luke's house.

"Good morning, could I please talk to Luke?" I asked when Luke's mom answered my knock.

She popped open the screen door, "Of course, honey. Come inside." She was still smiling as she climbed the carpeted steps. She must know about our dating secret by now, too.

I turned my attention to the many trinkets his mom had collected over the years. Tiny crystal animals, ceramic people doing different poses, and even some salt and pepper shakers from Europe, all in the large curio cabinet in the entryway hall.

My favorite things in the short hallway to the kitchen were the years of family photos hanging on the wall. Little Luke was so cute throughout the years.

It was early, and there was clamoring coming from somewhere on the second floor. A smile broadened across my face at the thought of him in his pajamas, rushing to get dressed.

Luke jumped down the stairs two by two and rushed over and scooped me up in a hug. His arms enveloped me just tight enough to hold me off the ground and make me relax into his scent. He peppered me with little kisses on my neck. He put me down and we had a deep, long kiss. His hands were on my cheeks and into my hair. I could feel his heart beating in my hands on his chest. We couldn't take our eyes off each other as we stumbled to the couch.

"Did your parents tell you I came by?" he asked shyly.

"My mom only told me this morning, and only because I asked," I said and remembered I was upset. "How could she just let me pine all these days?"

"You were pining?" he asked, and color came to my cheeks. He continued, "That's pretty mean of them. I was going to come over again, but Tom stopped me. He said I may make things worse. I have been just sitting here, going to work when I had to, and worrying about you, about us." He was sitting forward, looking at his hands. "I don't have any words to explain how scared I was to see you hurt like that."

"It was an accident. I don't blame you," I said as I scooted closer, wrapped my good arm through one of his arms, and rested my head on his shoulder. "I was scared for you, too. As soon as I was awake, I asked how you were."

"I had a pretty sore neck and my rib cage still aches, but you got the worst of it." His free hand reached across his body and rested on my head. We remained there together, close, and quiet for a few minutes.

After a bit, he said, "There was something I was going to tell you that day." He leaned back onto the couch cushions and fidgeted with his fingernails. I turned toward him, grabbed a throw pillow to prop up my cast, and waited for him to go on. "I love you, and I want us to be together forever," he said.

I swatted my cast at his chest and interlaced my undamaged fingers with his. "I know that," I said with relief. "We say that all the time." A flutter started in my chest and moved quickly to a rushing sound in my ears. I cocked my head. "Is there more?"

"Well, I know my mother won't have enough money to pay for college and I have little hope of having a good enough job to support a family without it."

Family? My muscles became tense and the baby-fine hairs on the back of my neck stood up. *What was he telling me?*

"In the fall, instead of going back to school, I'm going to join the Army." The words tumbled out of him.

My eyes grew wider and wider.

"I will be gone for a while," he continued. "You will graduate in two years and then we can get married. Your dad said you have to finish high school." Luke took our interlaced fingers to his chest. "We could live on base together."

I let go of his arm and sat with my back on the couch.

"It really won't be that long," he said. "I'll visit when I can, and we'll write like crazy."

Luke's eyes searched my face for some reassurance. I had none. "You're leaving? You're not finishing school?" I said with tears starting in my eyes. "This is just an idea, right?" I felt sick.

"I was thinking of our future. I signed up a few days before the accident," he said with a crack of hurt in his voice.

"You did this *before* the accident?" I was standing now. He was silent, staring at me with his pleading, nearly golden eyes. "We are just kids. I still have two years of school. Why wouldn't you ask me about this? What have you done?"

I shook my head, my palms pressed to my forehead. Memories of the day when I was seven and taken from my childhood home, and the day I was adopted filled my head. No one asked me, no one considered what I wanted. I flopped onto his couch and curled into a ball. Luke was hugging my whole body with his long arms. I barely felt him there.

Why can't my life go the way I want?

I went numb, and the tears stopped. It wasn't Luke's fault. Something inside me clicked. Maybe it was a breaking point; maybe it was something falling into place. *I was the one who would choose how my life went.*

I dried my eyes, unfurled myself, and looked at Luke sitting there next to me. "I won't wait." The words coming out of my mouth sounded too cold, but I went on. "This was the wrong call. This is not what I want. You should have talked to me first."

I left. He didn't follow. I walked into town passing the soda shop. Laura and Sarah Jane sat at the counter with Joe. I quickened my pace before they saw me. I wanted this hurt to be mine, for now.

What just happened? For better or worse, my life had just changed in ways I couldn't predict.

It was almost dark when I got home. Tom had already told Mom what happened. I was glad she knew. I apologized for being gone so long and walked to my room. I laid with my knees to my chest and my cast over them.

In the morning, outside my window, Mom's garden tomatoes were peeking from the dark cover of their leaves. Other large green leaves traveled up poles for beans, and squash plants abounded everywhere else. Everything ripe was waiting for her and Judy to come and pluck them before the day got too hot. For months I longed for my bedroom window to face the other direction, toward Luke's house. Today, I was relieved it didn't.

Yesterday morning, I wondered where Luke was and why he hadn't come to see me after the accident. The memory of walking out on Luke yesterday made me tear up again, sending me back into the darkness under my quilt. I tossed and turned with hot feelings of, *how could he,* then back to, *maybe I can fix this,* then right around to, *this is not what I want.* I stayed in my room most of the day.

Chapter Twelve

Before it seemed possible, school was about to start. I was sitting on the loveseat in our den like a stone. My knees were to my chest and my arms hugged them tight. Mom was sitting on the armchair knitting as she does in the afternoon between lunch and the next laundry load.

Earlier Tom told Mark, loud enough for me to hear, about Luke leaving at six tomorrow morning.

"Mom," I said, my eyes still on the carpet, "Did you ever have a broken heart? Was there anyone before Dad?" I put my cheek on my knee to face her. "Luke is leaving tomorrow, and I feel like there is more to say to him."

Mom set her knitting project in her lap. She looked out the window, choosing her next words carefully. "Beth, your father has always been the only one for me. I have loved him almost my whole life." Putting her project in the basket, she crossed to the loveseat and put her arm around me. "But there was a time he broke my heart."

"What happened?"

"You know your dad is older than me. He grew up just next door to me and Auntie Jillie," she paused. "And Ed." I flinched at the name of my biological father. Sometimes I forgot she was his sister. "I'm sorry to mention him, but if you want to know the story, he is involved."

"You can go on." I wanted to know about her life and sometimes that would involve Edward Dendin.

"Alright. Jillie and I are much younger than Ed, twenty-two years younger." My eyes raised to my hairline. "That's a story for another time," she said. "I was fifteen when I told John I loved him."

"You told *him*?" I shook my head with a smile wide across my face.

"Yes. He was nineteen, not dating anyone, and I wasn't sure if he was leaving after graduation. I knew I loved him and wanted only him forever."

"How could you know that at fifteen?"

"I just did." She closed her eyes with absolute resolution. "Stop interrupting. When I told him, I assured him I was not joking. He asked my father for permission to court me. He gave it. They knew he was good, and I was not silent about my love for him.

We dated a year before Ed came to visit." She sighed and sat back on the cushions of the couch. "Well, he did not approve. He said a twenty-year-old had no business being with a sixteen-year-old. Even though I was only two weeks from seventeen."

She saw I was about to interrupt again. She held up her hand. "Yes, it was the time just after Ed left your family, but I didn't know that."

She went on. "Your dad broke it off on the spot. My heart felt torn from my chest." Her hand came to her chest as if she could still feel it. "He left after that. Before he left, I saw him one more time. I needed him to know that I would always wait for him. There would never be another for me. He said that I should move on."

"After about a year, I heard John was learning to drive trucks and started working for a business a couple of towns over. I was almost eighteen then and had no other dates or suitors, and I still didn't want anyone but him.

"One Saturday I got on a bus and went to his workplace. I asked for him, but he wasn't there. They gave me his address, and I went to see him."

A smile spread across her face. "Boy, was he surprised to see me. He lived with two other young men. He grabbed his coat, and we walked down the street as I told him I still wanted to be with him no matter what my brother thought. Besides, Ed had run off months ago. John was quiet for a while. He was quiet even then.

"Then he said words I will never forget. 'It has always been you for me. No matter what it takes, I will marry you.'"

She stopped for a moment to savor her memory. "He spoke to my parents again. They said I must graduate and have one year of college. So I did what they asked to the letter and married your dad the day after that.

"Honey, I told you all that to tell you this. If you feel there are words left to say to Luke, you need to go say them. No matter what they are." She smoothed my hair with her hand.

Sitting there staring at the patterns the shag made on the rug, I decided I couldn't leave things this way, but what could I say to him? I popped off the loveseat and walked out the door.

"Thanks, Mom." I called back as I left. I walked down the street to Luke's door. I knocked softly. *Maybe no one would hear me. At least I could say I tried.* The door swung open and there he was, standing, staring at me.

"What are you doing here?" he asked. "Um, well, I mean, Hi. I'm just surprised to see you."

"I know. I'm sorry to just barge in like this," I said. "Can I talk to you for a minute on the porch?" The thought of being inside with him was too confining.

He came out and closed the door behind him.

"Look, I have been thinking about this for a while now," I started, and then took a deep breath.

"I'm so glad you were thinking about our future when you signed up for the Army. I don't really know what you've been doing these weeks besides basketball with my brother. I'm sorry I've treated you so badly."

"That's alright," he said and reached out for me.

Moving back, I laced my hands behind me. "I just wanted to come by to say I'm sorry," I said, looking down at the concrete steps. He sighed.

"I see. I was hoping this would go differently when I saw you at the door." He turned and put his hand on the door. "I guess I'll see you around," he said and walked back inside.

I left, wondering if I would ever see him again.

49 Years Ago

Chapter Thirteen

On the first week back from Christmas break, there were big signs all over for prom. Last year I went to Junior Prom with Buddy Harvey. He was tall and had glasses. He was super funny and a great kisser, even with those braces. This year I wanted to go with Joe. I knew he wasn't seeing anyone at the moment, so I thought it was a good time to ask. I was pretty bold and outspoken, especially with my friends. I called him up. "Hi Joe. Would you go to prom with me?"

"Gee, I just thought you were calling to go get a soda or something. You never hold back, do you?" I could hear the smile in his voice. "Yes, of course. I would love to go to prom with you."

"Fantastic! And now that you mention it, you want to go get a soda?" We laughed, and he agreed. "Meet you there in a bit." I hung up the phone.

When the phone rang seconds later, I answered, thinking it was Joe, but there was a woman on the other end. "Hello, does a girl named Beth live here?"

"I'm Beth. How can I help you?" It was unusual for me to get calls from people I didn't know.

"Sorry to just call like this but," long pause. "Well, this is Patty. Do you remember me? I'm your sister."

The word sister dampened my eyes and stung my nose. I had long since forgiven my older sisters for not telling me I would be taken away. I had always hoped someday to find them somehow. "Patty! I can't believe it. How did you know my number?" Both my hands clasped around the receiver, desperate for her answer.

"Well, Millie has correspondence with Auntie Joan once a year or so to let her know you guys are alright." Another long pause. I wanted to fill the gap with words, but there were too many thoughts racing through my head to choose.

My open smile hung on her next words. She continued, "I wrote Joan a letter telling her where I was, and I was hoping to find you guys. She sent a letter to Millie, and Millie said I could call sometime."

"She never mentioned it."

"She probably didn't want to get your hopes up. Maybe she thought I wouldn't call."

"I think of you from time to time, wondering what you are doing."

"I live in New York City, but I am visiting someone that lives near your town. We could meet up if you were willing."

"You're kidding! I would love that," I said, shocked at the prospect of seeing my sister again.

"Please tell the others they are welcome to come, but Mark, Debbie, and Donna's adopted parents don't want them to know." I rolled my eyes, knowing that was something Jillie would say.

After telling her Tom had gone back to college after winter break, we made plans to meet at Popsy's for lunch at noon the next day. We said goodbye, and I hung up the phone. Mom was out shopping, so I went to meet up with Joe like I had planned. I didn't tell him about Patty's call.

When I got home, Mom was in the kitchen making dinner. I went and sat at the table. "How was the store?" I asked, tapping my index finger on the table.

"Fine thanks. A little crowded." She placed the ground chuck into the bowl with breadcrumbs and spices and asked, "What have you been up to?" as she cracked an egg into the bowl.

"I went to have a soda with Joe." I paused, then went on, "Before I left, I got a call from Patty." Millie's hand froze deep in the ground meat and spices. Raising her eyebrows, she looked at me and swallowed hard.

"I was wondering if she would call. I haven't known for a long time. I was hoping to talk to her first. Are you okay?"

"I'm okay. Surprised, though." Looking at my hands, "Why didn't you tell me she might call?"

"I am sorry. Your father doesn't even know. I just wasn't sure she would go through with it." Taking her hands out of the bowl and wiping them on the kitchen towel, she sat at the table. "I didn't want to get your hopes up. I know how hard it is, even now, to call your family downstairs cousins."

I looked up at her, then down again at my hands. "Yes, but I get it now." I picked at my pink nail polish. "She asked me to meet her tomorrow. I told her we could have lunch at Popsy's."

Mom's eyebrows were up again. I could tell she was choosing her words carefully. "You're eighteen and graduating soon. You are old enough to make that decision. If you want, I could come for support."

“I think I’ll do this on my own.” I could see the hint of disappointment she tried to hide behind her smile.

Raising to the meatloaf bowl again, “Great, I hope it goes well. You could write and tell Tom.” Her back was turned to me. “But please don’t tell Judy just yet. After you meet up and see how things go, then we can tell her if you think we should.” I agreed. “Is there anything you were hoping to have as a side for the meatloaf?”

Ah yes, *the pretend it never happened and change the subject maneuver*, I knew it well. I played along and jumped from the table to grab the potatoes from the closet. “How about mashed potatoes and buttered carrots?” My mom nodded her head.

As I peeled the potatoes, I hit her with my own subject change. “Joe and I are going to prom together.” Relieved to have something else to talk about, we planned out all the details of prom shopping.

Chapter Fourteen

I recognized Patty instantly through Popsy's giant plate glass. She sat at a window seat searching passersby for some hope of recognition. It occurred to me she may not recognize me. It had been over ten years since the last time she saw me. Our eyes locked, and she stood up at the table. Tiny little bumps made my arm hair stand up under my many layers. I rubbed them down, crossed the road, and hopped the snowbank.

I burst into the diner, sending the bell over the door into a wild chime alerting all diners to my appearance. Patty met me there with a bear hug of an embrace.

"I'm so happy you're here. Thank you so much for meeting me," she said. She never asked where anyone else was. She was just happy to see me.

Holding hands, we walked to the table Patty had chosen. Before we could even ask how the other was, our waitress was at our table for our order. She was chewing her gum with her whole mouth, jaw opening wide, tongue moving, teeth chomping, and lips smacking. "What can I get ya?"

"Get whatever you want, Beth. I've got it covered."

"Um, a burger and fries. Oh, and a Coke, thanks," I said.

"And for you, big spenda?"

Patty snorted a laugh. "Same, please. Except for the Coke, could I get black coffee?"

"Sure thing." With that, the waitress clomped back behind the counter to call our orders back to the cook.

Patty pulled out her cigarette case and unlocked the brass clasp, lighting it with the matching brass lighter. She put the now lipstick-stained cigarette in the ashtray. She held out the case for me. "No thanks," I said, even though I wanted one.

She put the case away and looked me over with wide eyes. "You're so gorgeous. You must have the boys worshiping at your feet."

I reddened with a wide smile. "I have a few tortured followers." I put my nose in the air and my hand to my hair to hold my pretend crown. We both laughed.

"You're beautiful, too. Your hair is amazing." She had the cutest pixie cut. So bold and short with the most colorful thin headband tied across her forehead. "I never imagined you this way."

"The short hair was an impulse." Her hands touched the tips of her hair. "We were at a rally a few months ago and I chopped off my ponytail as an act of solidarity. A woman there was getting bullied by some men because of her short hair. I just happened to have scissors in my bag so…"

She paused and put her hands to her head and faked cutting off her ponytail. "I threw my hair at the guys, and I handed off the scissors. A bunch of other women did it too. When we got home, Betty fixed it up like this and I have grown to love it. It sure makes wig changes easier." She smiled and took off her winter coat. "I also burned my bra that day." With a laugh, she shook her shoulders, sending her ample chest every which way.

We both giggled and then she turned serious. Folding her arm on the table, she leaned in.

"I'm just going to jump right in," Patty said. "I know you are well cared for and I considered not calling at all. When the opportunity came up to see my friend in a town near here, I took it as a sign. Back when you were taken, I was so distraught, but there was nothing I could do about it. A sixteen-year-old is in no position to care for six children. I couldn't stand being in the house with *her*," she said, meaning our biological mother. "Not that she was there very much. I had always planned to leave for New York City after I graduated. I decided I could not stay there another minute. It took me two weeks to get a plan together and supplies. I convinced Betty to come too.

"I'm sorry I never came before. For a while, I didn't contact anyone. I was angry and felt useless to help." Patti reached across the table and took my hand. "I never stopped thinking about any of you."

Tears encroached on my sight, but I blinked them away. "I believe you Patty," I said, squeezing her hand back. "I was angry for a long time, too. I'm better now. Please go on, I want to hear about your adventure."

"Betty and I got to New York City with just enough money to pay rent for one room in a boarding house for one week. We immediately found waitress jobs and tried out for every play we could. Our combined tips and pay covered the rent for the room and we lived there a long time. We got small parts from time to time. We had no money for extras, but we were used to that." We both rolled our eyes, knowing the conditions we grew up in. "We were best friends and loved living and working together. We would rehearse scenes together, and the diner we worked at gave us one free meal at the end of our shift. Most days, it was the only meal we ate."

The waitress brought our food and drinks. Patty shifted the conversation, asking about me and the others. As I shoved fries in my mouth, I told her some about the orphanage and being adopted by John and Millie. I wasn't sure what she already knew, but she listened intently to every word.

I told her about running away and how after the last time's threat I saw that the Shelby's really wanted to love us and grow as a family, and how it took baby steps. "But I'm in a good place with them now. Judy, on the other hand, well, real damage was done in the orphanage at a tender age for her. I don't know if she'll ever let someone love her."

I told Patty about Luke and the accident. Then, feeling pretty drained, I turned to a lighter note and told her about Joe and the prom. "Oh my goodness, there he is!" I directed her eyes to the boy crossing the street. "That's Joe."

Our eyes followed the dapper young man in his stylish winter coat and hat. His hands were jammed in his pockets, and he bounced, waiting for the traffic to clear so he could finish his journey. Patty commented on how handsome he was. "Do any of your friends know about how your life was before you came here?"

"They know I was adopted, but no one has dug into it." Joe saw us sitting in the window and waved. He jumped the snowbank and popped inside.

With the jingle of the bell hanging over the door, my hands shook, so I hid them under the table. I wished I could hide all of myself. *What was I going to say?*

"Hello ladies," Joe said with a cheerful smile.

"Hey there Joe," I said, a little shaky. I started to introduce Patty when she stood up and cut me off.

Sticking out her hand, she spoke. "I'm Patty, an old friend of Beth's. I've just come for a visit from New York."

Hanging my head, I took a second while they shook hands. It was one thing not telling my friends about my old life; It was another thing to lie to their face. Feeling completely naked, I stood up with my hands on the table and my eyes closed. "Joe, this is not just my friend. Patty is my older sister." I opened one eye. There was shock on his face, but he smiled.

"I am so happy to meet you!" He turned back to Patty. "Beth said she was adopted, but I never wanted to pry."

"Would you like to join us?" I asked. He hung his coat on the hook at our seat and sat in the booth next to me. "Pry away," I said with a flourish of my hand.

Boy, did he ever. He asked Patty and I loads of questions, and we answered them as best we could. Even the biggie, "Why did your parents give you up?"

Patty had a better answer than mine. "My father is dead. Beth's abandoned us. I think our biological mother, Lizzy, is a woman who never received the right kind of love and, therefore, doesn't understand how to give love like a mother should," she said.

He seemed satisfied with that. Joe answered the questions Patty had for him, too. He turned the conversation to his thoughts on the upcoming prom and how he and the girls had been friends with me since my first day of school here. As we talked, my muscles relaxed and there was a feeling of warmth spreading through my body.

Eventually, Joe had to move on to his errand that brought him into town. "It was really nice to meet you," he said, shaking Patty's hand. He looked at me. "I'll call you later." He put his coat on and headed out.

"Boy, what a looker. Any sparks there?" Patty asked after the bell announced his departure.

"Nothing like that. We're just friends."

"Hmmm." She looked at me with a raised eyebrow.

I turned the question back to her. "What about you? Are there men falling all over you and Betty in the big city?"

She shifted in her seat a bit. "Well," she took a sip of the coffee the waitress had just refilled with the big glass coffee pot. "Betty and I focus on our acting. We aren't looking for anyone to take us from that."

She did, however, have all the gossip about my sisters. She reconnected with Barb, and Barb knew about everyone. My sister Mary had died along with her husband when they were twenty-seven in a bar brawl they may have started. Her children lived with Barb after that.

Barb was doing well with Tommy. He owned Shelly's diner now, and they ran it together. Sarah and Kathy were the same as they had always been, drinking, baby-making machines.

She plopped her suitcase of a purse onto the table. "I was hoping you would be interested in seeing these." She pulled out the crown jewels of history: photos.

My eyes sparkled as I looked over the black-and-white images on thick paper. Everyone posed, one in front of the other, or babies on their parent's laps.

"How did you get these?" I asked, as I studied them one by one.

"Joan."

"This looks like how I remember the house in New Hampshire"

"That *is* the house." She gave a brilliant smile.

"Who are these kids? Is this one me?" I pointed to a little girl no older than two.

"Yes, and this is Tom, Mark, and me." She pointed to them all. "There are more. Keep looking."

There were ones with Kathy, Sarah, Barb, and Patty all in a row. A couple with Lizzy and the younger kids. Then one that made my eyes sting. "Is this me and Ed?"

"Ya."

Setting the photo down on the table, I sat back against the booth's hard vinyl. "I don't think of him much anymore." I closed my eyes. "You know that Millie and Jillie are his sisters." I looked at her. She nodded. "He is nowhere to be found."

"It's true. No one knows where he is. Ed really disappeared." She reached out to collect the pictures.

"Sometimes I don't understand people."

"Me either." Patty lingered over the picture of Ed and me. "You have his eyes, you know?"

"I noticed that. And Lizzie's cheeks." My hands cupped my round cheeks and blew them big with air. We both laughed.

The biggest news of the day was that there were siblings younger than Judy. Auntie Joan knew Lizzy had brought five more babies into the world before an accident made it impossible for her to have any more children. Lizzy gave them all up at birth, not even caring to look at them.

As we stood to leave, we exchanged addresses promising to write at least once a month faithfully.

We hugged and cried and dallied and finally parted at four o’clock.

Chapter Fifteen

In the weeks leading up to prom, Mom and I filled our days with dress shopping, only finding the perfect one a week before the big event. This year's prom theme was "Out of this World". My dress swirled with blues, purples, and sequins. It looked like galaxies full of stars.

My mother and I stood and looked at the dress together side by side. Her hands were on my shoulders. We peered into the mirror; our faces close together. I saw Ed's eyes on Millie. *How did I never notice?*

"We have the same eyes," I said without thinking.

Mom hugged my shoulders tighter and closed her eyes. "I know. It was the first thing I noticed when I saw you," she said.

"Why didn't you say anything?"

"I didn't want to remind you of Ed. He really did a number on us both." She sat in a plush chair next to the floor to ceiling mirrors.

I stepped off the little stage the store had with surrounding mirrors. "I love having features the same as yours. It reminds me we are truly family."

With that, tears fell down both of our cheeks. I crouched beside her chair and hugged her neck. She reached her arms around me the best she could in our awkward position and leaned her head on mine.

"I love you Beth," she said.

"I love you too, Mom.

Chapter Sixteen

Also in the weeks leading up to prom, Joe started coming over to visit me more than usual. He walked me home and asked me out for sodas by myself, but never once tried to kiss me. We just talked. We talked about Patty and other parts of my life before. We talked about our futures, our favorite TV shows, and juicy gossip. He was still just a friend, but something had changed for me. He had become closer. Maybe it was just my family secret we shared.

Prom night, I stepped my feet into my dress and pulled it on. My bouffant hairdo made it impossible to get it on over my head. I slid purple eyeshadow on my eyelids and drew on thick black eyeliner that winged out the edge across my lids. My mother's hands were as shaky as mine when she helped me put on the long black eyelashes. I noticed tears in her eyes.

"Mom, are you crying?" I asked.

She took a deep breath. "I never thought your father and I would have children," she said. "You, your brother, and your sister have been such a blessing to me. Even when times were tough in the beginning, I loved having you." She sat on the edge of the bed near my vanity. "When we heard you and your siblings had been taken from Lizzy, I wanted to come for you right away, but it took some convincing." Her eyes fluttered toward the hall.

Mom continued. "We had just gotten the news from the doctor that I would likely never have children because of certain," she paused, "womanly issues Jillie and I share." She blushed and turned away. "Anyway, I guess I'm just feeling grateful." I reached across to hug her, careful not to smudge my makeup, and we sat together a minute before she sniffled and said, "Let's finish you up. Joe will be here soon."

She wasn't wrong. Just ten minutes later, Joe rang the doorbell. I was in the living room when he came up the stairs. *Doesn't he look great in that suit?*

The lavender cumber bun around his waist and bow tie set off his blue eyes, and I loved the white jacket. His smile widened when he saw me.

"Wow!" he said, scanning me from head to toe. "You look great." He went to my father and shook his hand. "Good evening, Mr. Shelby. Thanks for letting me take Beth to prom tonight."

My dad seemed pleased by this–I could tell by the slight weakening of the scowl on his forehead, imperceptible to anyone else but me. "Have her home by midnight, son," he said smoothly with an implied *or else.*

"Yes, sir." He turned to my mother. "Doesn't Beth look wonderful?" he asked her.

"Yes, beautiful," she said.

I became uncomfortable with everyone looking at me. I turned to Joe and said, "Okay, we should go and meet the others." I grabbed my shawl.

"Wait, I almost forgot. This is for you." He handed me the box he had been holding under his arm.

It was a corsage with beautiful pink and purple flowers. Joe popped open the box and slid the bouquet on my wrist.

"Isn't it lovely?" Mom said. "Those lilies and irises are rare this time of year," she said with a nod, clearly impressed that Joe would be so thoughtful.

Everyone was smiling. Well, everyone but my dad. But he wasn't scowling quite so much. My mom snapped some pictures before we left.

Before the prom, we met the gang at Popsy's Burgers downtown at six o'clock. Napkins covered our satin and taffeta. Burgers were bitten over plates and fries were poked with forks. Gasps came from all around when Sarah Jane had a red blob of ketchup fall from her fry to the napkin in her lap. No one breathed as she lifted it onto the table and replaced it with a clean one. Tragedy averted.

After dinner, Joe and I got into his dad's Buick and the others went in their own cars. We started towards the school; the prom was in the gym. Two blocks before the school, Joe turned down Webb Road. Confused at first, I went with it. Maybe he had some bottle of something we could sip before the dance, or maybe he finally wanted to make out.

Joe parked the car and cut the engine. He looked at me, then at the steering wheel. There was a long silence. Joe was never shy with me.

"Joe, what's going on here?" I asked.

"I need to tell you something," he said. "Something I have never told anyone, but I need you to know. You shared something amazing and personal with me when you told me about Patty. We have talked and become even closer than ever these last few weeks." Then he stopped talking again and stared at the steering wheel.

Turning toward him, "Well?" I asked when I couldn't take it anymore.

"Well, I felt I should tell you I love you more than any other girl, but I could never be more than your friend."

"What? Why would you say that? We have been talking and have been closer than ever lately. You said it yourself. We talk about everything, and you have never even tried to—" Something dawned on me. "Oh," I said, and sat back against the car door.

I could see him blushing, even in the dimly lit car. He looked at me from the corner of his eye, not able to fully turn to me. Many things went through my head in a flash, *I had heard of this*, *Why did it have to be him*, And then, at the end of a thousand other thoughts that came and went like lightning, *He took a big risk telling me*, *He must really trust me.*

"Thanks for telling me." I said, and I reached my hand out to touch his shoulder. "I understand, and it's okay with me."

His head went gently to the steering wheel, and I could see silent tear drops falling in the streetlamp's light. A relieved set of quiet tears you cry when you realize someone loves you for who you are.

"I have only let myself believe it and accept it a couple of months ago. I am going off to college in August and I don't know what to do. Throughout high school, I have tried, struggling, to be normal. Trying to find a girl that I could settle down with and forget about my feelings toward boys. I was hoping maybe that was you, but I understand now it could never make me truly happy and it wouldn't be fair to you. He wiped his eyes. "I probably don't have to say this, but please don't tell anyone else. Not even Joanie knows."

"Are you kidding me?" pushing at his shoulder. "We're secret keepers now. I'd never tell." I took his face and pointed it at me. "Your secret is safe with me. In fact, if you wanted to continue to date me this summer, just to make things look good, that would be fun."

"You would do that for me?" he said, his eyes wide. "But don't you want to find a boyfriend that could actually marry you someday?"

"That will come in its own time," I said. "I haven't been interested in marriage at all or even any serious boyfriend since Luke. Maybe it's silly, but he's still at the center of my heart."

We hugged, and I kissed him on the cheek. "Let's go dance!" I flicked my bouffant hairdo.

"You've got it," he said and started the car up again.

At prom, I countered the "What took you guys so long?" question with wide, true smiles at Joe that showed we shared something intimate. The girls responded with giggles and rushed me off to the dance floor. We danced and laughed and drank punch all night long.

Exhausted, the night finally came to the last song. Joe asked me to dance. We swayed to Ben E. King singing Stand by Me. After the last dance, all of us were hugging and saying our goodbyes. I had a moment of realization that the class of 1964 would never be together like this again.

Joe was pretty quiet on the way home. When he pulled up to my house, he said, "Thanks for tonight, Beth. Is it okay if we're friends just like always? I don't want to pretend we are dating. We can still have a bunch of fun this summer," he said.

"Of course." I gave him another big hug, and he jumped out of the car and came around to open my door.

He walked me up my steps and kissed me on the cheek. "You're the best friend I've ever had. See you around."

I watched him walk back down the concrete steps. As he came to the bottom, he grabbed the wrought-iron railing and hopped down the last two. Jumping into the car through the window, he started the engine and drove off.

Upstairs, Mom and Dad were in their armchairs. She was knitting and he was watching the late news.

"You look like you had a good time," Mom said, commenting on the smile I was wearing ear to ear.

"I'm glad you're home on time," Dad said. I looked at the clock. It was midnight on the nose. Lucky for me, Joe must have been keeping track.

"It was the best. We danced all night." I hummed as I waltzed across the living room. "I'm tired now, though. I'm going to get cleaned up and go to bed." I hugged them both and walked down the hall to my room.

I stopped at Judy's open door and peeked in. There was no movement in her bed. I turned to leave, but a whisper broke the stillness. "Did he kiss you?" She popped her whole torso up from under the covers, greedy for details.

"A lady shouldn't kiss and tell," I said and wiggled my eyebrows and gave her a wink to make her think something happened worth keeping a secret. She sighed and fell back onto her pillow. "Goodnight," I said to her and walked down the hall.

I stood in my room after I washed my face and pulled on my soft pajamas. I went over the night in my head as I brushed out all the hairspray from my hair. What an amazing secret to have with someone. I hope someday he will have the kind of love he deserves.

Chapter Seventeen

Joe and the rest of us had an amazing summer together, with a blur of swimming, camping, and drive-in movies. All of us together: Joe, Joanie, Sarah Jane and her boyfriend Sam, Laura and her boyfriend of the week. Even Laura's brother, Matt, tagged along sometimes.

If Matt was there when we piled into someone's car, I made sure to be on his lap. If Matt was with us at the lake, I would park my towel beside his.

August had arrived. Joe and Sarah Jane had left for college the week before, and there was a great big hole in my heart for them both.

Laura's house always made me breathe easy. In winter, the roaring fireplace wrapped around me like a fuzzy blanket, and in summer, the ceiling fans blew sweet relief to my sizzling skin.

Today, Elvis was wafting to my ears as I sat on the green velvet couch, one of three in the room. My fingers mindlessly moved back and forth on the fabric, changing its sheen from dull to shiny and back again. Laura was lying across the smaller velvet loveseat. It was the kind of tranquil afternoon you didn't know you would miss someday.

It all ended when Matt threw open the front door. "I have arrived," he said, spreading his arms royally. He closed the front door, spun around, and long-jumped over Laura's couch, which he easily cleared, and landed on his feet just inches from my feet.

Terrified he would land on me, I stood, trying to get out of the way. I wasn't quick enough, so I braced for impact.

He came to an abrupt halt. We stood nose to nose. "Gee Beth, why so jumpy?" he said, inches from my face. The effect of his closeness made me thankful there was a couch to melt back onto.

Matt Bonnet was the whole package. Blonde locks that were the perfect kind of curly to tangle your fingers in. His blue eyes literally stopped some people in their tracks. His build was strictly model material. Everyone who saw him fell in love instantly. He would go back to his last year of college in a couple of weeks to finish his accounting degree.

"Hi," I said. I flashed my coolest smile. He plopped himself beside me, stretching his arms wide. I could feel the heat of his arm behind my damp neck.

"Laura, can you get me a soda?" He jerked his head towards the kitchen door.

Laura gave an exaggerated sigh and headed into the kitchen. Once the swinging door finished swishing behind her, Matt turned to me. I flushed but leaned toward him. "Hi," I said. "This is new." My eyes gestured to his arm around me.

"Ya," he said, "I've been watching you this summer."

"You like what you see?" I asked.

With a raise of his eyebrows and a smile, he kissed me. A deep, powerful kiss that had been practiced before. Even sitting down, I could feel my knees buckling and my thighs melting into the sofa. His kiss was guiding me down into an almost horizontal position on the big comfy couch. My head swirled.

The sound of Laura busting back in through the swinging door with a tray of sodas for all of us brought me back to reality.

"Whoa!" she stopped short in the middle of the shag carpet and almost spilled the drinks. I was on the other side of the couch in half a second, straightening my shirt and hair. "Matt, stop messing with my friends. Take your soda and go upstairs," she said. Matt grabbed the soda, winked at me, and bound up the stairs two by two.

"Wow, sorry," I said. "That just kinda happened."

"That's okay. I don't mind if you kiss my brother. I just don't want you to get hurt. He's kind of a good time boy. He says he has lots of girlfriends at school."

"Thanks, I'll keep that in mind." I fixed my hair and took a sip of soda. Matt didn't come down the rest of the afternoon and I went home wanting more.

Two days later, in my new miniskirt, I rang Laura's bell at about noon. Matt swung the door wide and backed up to let me in.

"Laura's not here. She went to the pool with my mom," He told me as he shut the door behind me.

"Oh ya. She told me, but I forgot." *I did not.* I had always had a thing for Matt and now that he showed some interest, I was hoping to have a little fun. I turned to leave, hoping he would say something.

"Hey, but I'm here and if you want to stay and wait, that would be okay." *Bingo.* He walked to the olive green couch. He sat down and motioned for me to join him.

"Is your dad here?"

"Nope, the poor fella had to go to work," he said, lacing his fingers behind his head. I smoothed my sweaty palms on my skirt. *Of all the questionable decisions I have made.* I moved across the room and sat down. He was twenty-two, and I still felt like a kid. *What exactly was I looking for here?*

"Look," I said, getting cold feet, "tell Laura I'll see her tomorrow."

"Don't go." He took my hand. "I want to talk a bit. We've been having fun this summer, but we've never just talked. I want to know you better." His words fell over me like silk. "Laura told me you're gonna start working soon." My face reddened. It seemed like he was really interested in me.

"Well, I'll be working at Dr. Massie's office next week as a receptionist. I still live with my folks and these next few weeks I plan to have as much fun as I can squeeze out of summer."

"What about a boy?" he asked, looking me straight in the eyes. "Is there anyone special?"

"No. Do you have anyone waiting back at school?"

"No." His hand gliding up my arm came to rest on my shoulder. He drew me close for another of those deep kisses that melted. Kissing him back, I wrapped my arms around his torso. Things fell into place like a dream, as they did yesterday. His fingers in my hair, one arm wrapped around me, pulling me close, then guiding me down to the couch cushions. We were lying side by side as best we could before we came up for air.

"Hi." He smoothed my hair from my face.

"Hi," I said with a little laugh.

"This okay?"

"Yes."

He brought me in for another kiss. He reached under my shirt, and I let him.

Minutes lingered while we explored each other thoroughly. Our bodies were as close as they could be, and I could feel how engaged he was. Matt slid his hand down my thigh and bent my leg around his. On his way up from my knee, I felt my skirt rise. He moved his hand between my thighs, and again, I let him.

I was brought slightly back into reality by the slow ticking of Matt unzipping his pants. "Matt, I have never gone that far before."

"It feels so good, so much better than this." He came back down and kissed my neck. "I really want you. You are so beautiful." His soft words put me back in a trance.

"Okay," I moaned, "but—," was all I said before he kissed me again.

He was right, this felt better. Fearful of opening my eyes and seeing *it*, I kept them closed.

Soon, I became oblivious to everything but the rush of blood in my ears and the breath that steamed our cheeks.

We moved in rhythm, back and forth. That ascending feeling I only had alone in my room was coming to a peak right here with Matt. Every muscle in my body was engaged. My breath came in quick gasps. My legs grasped Matt tight, trying to get him closer to where I needed him to be. My eyes popped open, and I shook as pleasure shot through my body. Seconds later, Matt's face seemed to experience a similar pleasure.

Afterwards, he stroked the hair from my face and kissed my cheek. He mopped the sweat from his brow with the throw blanket on the back of the couch.

Then the gravity of the situation hit me. Thoughts started going through my head like bullets. *What did I do? How could I have let things go this far? We barely even like each other.* I scooched out from under him. I sat there and straightened my clothes. "That was amazing," I said. "But we probably shouldn't have done it." Tears welled in my eyes.

Matt put his arm around me. I tried to move away, but he held me still. "Look," he said. "I really like you. We didn't do anything wrong. These days it's not like it used to be. People are doing it all the time. I know loads of girls at school that have sex."

"So, you have done this before?" My eyes cast down at my hands.

"I won't lie to you, yes I have," Matt told me honestly. He caught my eye, "I really do like you."

It was getting easier to believe that I did nothing wrong. He kissed me and it was even easier.

Finally, I stood. There was a soreness between my legs. "I think I'd better go."

"Please stay. We can watch television. Laura really will be home in about an hour." He walked across the living room to turn on the TV.

"No thanks. I'll see you around." I felt like an idiot, but that is all that came out of my mouth. I turned to the door to go. Matt bounded across to meet me.

"Okay," he said as he opened the door, "but will you come back tomorrow?"

I brightened a bit at this. *Did he really want to see me again?* "What time?" I asked, smiling.

"Noon," he said, touching my chin. He lifted my face and kissed me.

"That sounds good. See you then." He kissed me again.

I walked home, every step in confusion. I couldn't feel comfortable with what had just happened, but I couldn't stop feeling the urge to do it again. By the time I got to my house, I had a smile on my face.

"I think I will take a bath to cool off," I told Judy as I crossed the living room.

"Have fun," she said sarcastically.

I already did. With a secret smile, I closed the bathroom door.

Chapter Eighteen

Matt and I never got another chance to be alone, but the time we spent together was fun and easy. He taught me to drive his stick shift. Hours of fits and starts and grinding gears until the car rode smooth enough to drive to Popsy's for a reward shake.

When we hung around at Matt's house, Laura would come behind us on the couch. She'd throw one arm around me and one arm around Matt and smoosh her face in between us. Sometimes, she and her beau of the week would meet us at the pool or double date at the drive-in.

I started my job at the dentist's office and Matt got ready to go back to school. Even though we shared my "first time," I wasn't very sad about him leaving, but I would miss him. We had fun the last few weeks, but it just served as a reminder that I didn't want anything serious.

Two days before Matt left for school, I stood at the kitchen sink with soap suds all over my hands as I washed the bowl and spoon I had used for my late breakfast. Standing there, a wave of nausea washed over me. Tiny cool beads of sweat formed on my forehead and upper lip. After I rinsed the dishes, I waited, holding the counter and my stomach.

"Are you feeling ill again?" Mom asked from the table where she was having a midmorning coffee break.

"Ya, it's weird. I don't usually get sick this time of year."

"I know, sickness only in the mornings too, weird." She said the last word pointedly.

I heard the word *morning* and put it together with *sickness*. As if all the bones disappeared from my body, I fell straight to the linoleum.

"Beth!" Mom dashed to my side.

She straightened me out on the floor and put my head in her lap. Giant tears fell from my eyes. I wrapped my arms around her waist.

"Oh, honey." She stayed there, smoothing my hair and loving me. "You're going to be okay," she said, which made me cry even more. "We'll figure it out."

Later, I stood there looking at the calendar like a fool. My heart fell into my stomach. Maybe I was wrong about when my last period started. *Are you kidding me?* I tried not to hyperventilate.

Twenty minutes later, I was knocking at Matt and Laura's door. One look at my puffy red eyes and he knew something was wrong. He guided me to the couch. Laura came through the swinging door and saw my face. As soon as she looked at me. "Hey," she said "What's going on? Shouldn't you be at work?" she asked before Matt could.

"I'm not feeling well," I said without looking at either of them.

"If you are not feeling well, why did you come here?" As soon as she asked the question, her hand went up in front of her mouth.

Things like this were not foreign to us. We've all heard the stories where girls would be sick and then have a six-month "vacation" at their grandma's. Some older girls would be single one day and married the next, claiming premature birth seven months later.

Wide-eyed she looked at Matt and then at me. "I will be in my room," she said. As she walked by Matt, she punched him in the arm and mouthed, *Stupid.* Matt only ruffled his brow and shrugged his shoulders.

Matt sat beside me. "Why *did* you come here if you didn't feel well?" he asked, truly confused.

"Because I'm not only sick," I said. "I'm late." I looked at him for some recognition. He fell back onto the cushion of the couch.

His hand on his stomach, "I think *I'm* going to be sick." He said and then started mumbling to himself.

My hand grazed his knee, and he flinched away. "We only did it once. How can you be, *you know*," motioning to my stomach with both hands. "We only did it once." He looked at me for an answer.

"I don't know, but I think I am." Curling my arms around my midsection, "I didn't even realize I was late until this morning." I grabbed the nearest throw pillow and face-planted into the back of the couch.

"I guess we should get married," he said.

My whole body stopped. I stopped crying. Stopped blinking. Stopped breathing. I ran to the bathroom and threw up again.

When I got back, he was still sitting on the couch. He was smiling, which made me smile. I was prepared to see him off to college on Friday, say goodbye, probably forever, and that was okay with me. We made no commitment to each other, and I didn't love him. But now, with all the emotions going on inside me, there was something comforting and safe in his smile.

What the hell am I going to do? I've never felt more like my mother than right now. I walked past him without responding and went to see Laura.

Laura was lying on her bed reading her cosmetology books. It was no surprise to anyone when she went to beauty school after high school.

"Hi," she said with a knowing grin. "So you and my brother have been closer than I realized this summer, huh?"

I produced a nervous smile. "I wanted to tell you, but it felt a little weird." I tinkered with the perfumes and little crystal animals on her dresser. "I don't know for sure that I am," I said, stopping short before the word pregnant.

"So, what's he going to do about it?" she asked. *What was he going to do?* It was the first time I realized it was not only my fault.

"He said we should get married." I scrunched up my face and turned to see her reaction.

She jumped off the bed and leaped toward me. "Sisters!" she shouted and wrapped her arms around my neck. Hugging her back, I thought a connection to this family wouldn't be so bad.

"I really don't know if I am. We will have to talk to our parents and go to the doctor's to be sure."

"How late are you?"

"Somewhere over two weeks."

"And you have been tossing your cookies the last few days?" She looked at me up and down. She said with an eye roll, "Oh yeah, we're going to be sisters." She laughed, and I felt sick again.

Our parents said all the things you could imagine parents saying. I even heard Matt's dad whisper in Matt's ear, "Son, are you sure it's yours?"

A doctor's trip later and our parents worked it all out for us as if we weren't even in the room. We would be married. I would live with Matt's parents and Matt would transfer to a closer school to commute for his last year. Matt seemed fine with this, but I protested.

I called Patty. "Beth, please come to us in New York. You need to know you have," she paused. "Options." A cold sweat broke out on my palms. All the girls knew what that meant, even the good girls. I told her I would think about it, and I did. In the day or so I considered it, my brain practically broke. The idea I could raise this baby on my own was never brought to my attention. My options were Matt, adoption, or a dirty room off some dark alley in the biggest city in the country.

One night I was sitting with my mom and her knitting. "I don't love him," I said in the middle of a *Bewitched* commercial break.

"You might learn to love him, dear." Taking one hand off her knitting, she touched my shoulder. "You don't have many choices here. He wants to do the right thing."

My hormones eventually swayed me into keeping the baby, which meant keeping Matt, too. We were married on October 16, 1964.

48 Years Ago

Chapter Nineteen

My stomach was bigger than I ever thought possible. Eight months pregnant and every day I put one foot in front of the other. Trying to pivot from a longtime friend to a live-in family member.

Matt and his parents convinced me to quit my job and take over most of the cleaning and cooking duties because both Mr. and Mrs. Bonnet work.

As we got closer to Matt's graduation, Matt heard about a job from a friend who worked as a hotel desk clerk. The Carlton Hotel was going to need an accountant. He could start right after graduation. The hotel was an hour away so it would be a hard commute before we got set up in our own place, but manageable.

At three o'clock in the morning on May fourth, I woke with extreme pain. My stomach and pelvis were on fire.

"What's wrong?" Matt asked. I lay there moaning, curled in a ball.

He ran from the room and returned with his parents. Matt grabbed my right arm, and his dad grabbed my left. They helped me to the door, down the stairs, and into the car. His mom tossed some things in a travel bag for me, and we were off to the hospital.

The nurses took me right in. During the exam, the doctor confirmed I was in labor. He grabbed the straw from my water cup, stuck it you know where, and broke my water. My mouth hung open in shock as he tossed the straw in the trash and told the nurse to call him when I was fully dilated.

Alone and in pain most of the day, it was six in the evening and the nurse was yelling at me to push. I did my best, but even the drugs didn't take this pain away. *How did people do this more than once?* I kept thinking. Yes, it was easy to dupe someone into this one time, but again? No way.

Thirty minutes of pushing later, I got my answer. The most amazing little person came out of my body and then nothing else mattered. The doctor held her high and said magical words, "It's a girl." I went from vessel to mother in an instant.

A nurse cleaned and wrapped her. I only took my eyes off my daughter for a moment when I felt a needle go into my arm. Next to my bed stood a different nurse with a syringe of something stuck inches deep into my arm.

She looked up at me, "You're not planning to breastfeed, are you?" she asked.

"I don't think so."

"Good," she said and proceeded to pump me full of whatever was in that syringe to prevent me from making breast milk.

With my eyes back on my baby, I watched as she was wiped, diapered, and swaddled. The nurse brought her to my arms. I kissed her forehead, her cheeks, and her little hands.

After my daughter and I were clean, the nurses let Matt in. He stopped at the doorway when he saw us. Tears were in his eyes when he got to our side. One hand on my shoulder and the other on her chest, he stood there entranced as he felt her breathing.

"Hold her." I moved my arms to lift her to him.

He hesitated a moment, then took her in his arms. Holding her with one arm and unwrapping her with the other, he inspected her tiny hands and feet and skinny little legs. Tears were still in his eyes when he looked back at me. "Should we name her Julie?" he asked.

"I've always loved that name." With tears in my eyes, too, I said, "Hello Julie," and waggled her foot.

When the nurse took Julie, Matt came over and climbed into the hospital bed with me. I laid my head in the crook of his arm where the baby had been. "Sorry you had to miss class," I said with a sleepy smile.

"Are you kidding me?" he asked, looking down at me to see if I was joking. "I'm happy I was there when you went into labor. I couldn't have even imagined how wonderful she is." I closed my eyes and slept.

Blessed to have Matt's parents help in the first weeks of Julie's life, I was still grateful we found an apartment as soon as Matt graduated. A two-bedroom on the first floor of a blue three-family house. The yellow kitchen was large and cheery. It came with a nice-sized kitchen table. Matt's parents let us have the green velvet couch, our bed, and Julie's new crib. The only things we had to buy were a highchair, dresser, and television. It was small, wonderful, and ours.

Chapter Twenty

When Julie was five months old, she had an ear infection. At three in the morning, she woke us for the third time. I rolled over and walked my fingers up Matt's back. "If you go put her back to sleep, I'll make it worth your while."

He groaned. He had come home late from work smelling of booze and perfume. Again.

"Come on, you never get up with her," I whined.

Matt flipped over to face me scowling, "I worked all day and have to go back tomorrow. Go and shut her up."

Raising my voice, "Maybe if you didn't stay out so late or drink so much, you'd be in better shape to help me out." I sat up on both elbows.

"She is your job," he said through his teeth, then shoved me with his foot.

"What the hell! Don't be an ass." I turned away and got up.

The heel of his foot connected with my lower back. He kicked me hard, pushing me right off the bed.

Matt laughed. "Sorry," he said. "I didn't know you were that close to the edge."

"Asshole! Yes, you did." I stood and swatted at him as he dove under the covers. Things like this were happening more often now that we lived alone. I left the room to get Julie.

45 Years Ago

Chapter Twenty-One

September has come, and it was almost my birthday. I woke up that morning and had a familiar feeling. After running into the bathroom to hug the toilet, I went to the calendar and realized, just as I had a year ago, that I was two weeks late for my period.

Jennifer came in May, a year after Julie. Then Jessica in August a year and a half after that. Once Jess was born, I vowed to be more careful in our lovemaking to take a break from baby making.

That was easier than I thought. About that time, Matt started staying out longer, and when he was home, he had no interest in me. There was always some reasonable excuse with work or his parents. Soon it became odd to see him home before I went to bed on a weeknight. On the weekends, we would go visiting. He was sweet as pie when people were around, so I made sure we went out every Saturday.

Chapter Twenty-Two

"Go shopping or visit Matt at work or something. Go get some fresh air. I will watch the girls," my mom suggested one day when she was visiting. When I hesitated, she grabbed my sweater and slapped her keys in my hand. "Go," she said.

I'd never been to see Matt at work. *It might be fun*, I thought as I drove.

As I walked into the Carlton Hotel, I caught sight of Matt sitting on the lobby couch next to a redhead. He had his arm over the back of the couch, and they were turned towards each other with coffee cups in their hands.

I stopped short just inside the door. The woman noticed me first and motioned for Matt to look. He scrambled up with bulging eyes and came over to me.

"Beth? What are you doing here? Is everything okay? Where are the girls?" He guided me to the couch on the other side of the lobby and sat me facing away from the redhead. He positioned himself across from me on the wooden coffee table.

"What did I just walk in on?" I asked, sounding more hysterical than I wanted to.

"Are the girls okay?" Matt asked again.

"Yes, they are with my mom. She thought it would be nice for me to get out," I said, trying to turn around. Matt put his hand on the side of my face, so I was looking at him again. "Answer my question. Who did you just have your arm around?"

He didn't respond right away. "That is Karen. She works at the front desk. I was consoling her because her mom is sick," he told me with his sincere face he usually keeps for others.

"She didn't look sad or upset to me. It looked like you two were having a grand time."

"That is because my cheering up worked. We were just about to get back to work when you came in," he said.

Side-eyed I asked, "Really?" He nodded his head, and I felt guilty. "Sorry, I got a little crazy."

"I'm sorry you misunderstood. It was all very innocent. Would you like to meet her?"

"No," I said. "I feel a little silly for the look I gave you two when I came in."

"I'm really sorry, but I should get back to work."

"Yes, of course," I said, grabbing my purse. "Mom gave me her car. I still need to go to the market." I turned and asked loud enough for the redhead to hear, "Will we see you for dinner?"

"Yes, I'll be home at about six. It will be nice to eat together. Sorry I have been having to work so much."

Sometimes I forget Matt's public persona. Collecting myself, I replied, "You have to do what you have to. Don't worry about us." I turned back to him, took a step closer, and put my hand on his chest. "But it would be nice to eat together. Maybe then we can watch a bit of TV as a family before the girls go to bed." I smiled, kissed his cheek, and walked out the door. As I walked back to the car, I knew I was being duped.

When Matt came home, all three girls were in the playpen. He came into the kitchen and laid his briefcase on the table. I didn't turn from my cooking until he grabbed my arm and spun me toward him.

He cupped my face in his hand. "Why were you at the hotel today?" he growled in a tone that didn't sound like his voice. His hand moved from my cheek into my hair. His fingers locked around my tendrils. My neck wrenched as he pulled my head down to my shoulder. "Checking up on me?" He squeezed my upper arm until I cried out. "Who do you think you are?"

I tried to sputter out answers I thought would calm him when the back of his hand came across my face. The force buckled my knees, sending me to the floor.

He shook his head as if waking up from a dream. "Beth, I'm sorry!" he said, and fell to the floor with me.

I kicked away from him with my feet until I hit the wall. He caught me and held me close through my protesting. Holding me fast, his apologetic tears started to fall. He blubbered things like: he was so sorry, he felt betrayed by my lack of trust, it made him crazy.

I convinced myself that this was all a big misunderstanding and somehow mostly my fault. Soon, both of us were crying and apologizing. We had sex right there on the floor. Afterwards, I got the girls from the living room and put dinner on the table. There were no more words between us for the rest of the night.

It took three days for the swelling to go down on my face and two more for my foundation to cover the bruise. I stayed inside the entire week until it could be explained away with a story about a rogue toy to the face. There had been pokes and pushes, but that was the first time he hit me.

Chapter Twenty-Three

It was June, and I felt that old familiar feeling. I stood at the stove cooking more eggs for Jess when I mentioned to Matt I may be pregnant.

He dropped his fork into his scrambled eggs. "We hardly even have sex anymore," he said.

"But we did a couple of weeks ago when you came home, don't you remember?" I turned to him. "Right there." I motioned to the corner of the kitchen. I tried to smile and pretend that night was no big deal. Jess was sitting in her highchair. The other girls were playing in the playpen in the living room.

Matt leaped from the table and crushed me against the Formica counter. "That is not funny," he said. My head was turned away and his nose was touching my cheek. "Are you having an affair?" he asked through his teeth.

"Of course not," I said. I tried to push him off with one arm, because my other one was pinned between us. "Are you kidding me? I never leave the house," I said, motioning to the room which sometimes felt like a prison. "Get. Off. Me," I said in his face.

He loosened the pressure as the eggs burned. I pushed him away, turned off the stove, and grabbed Jess. Tears streamed down my face as I walked to the living room.

He followed me with an apology. Saying things like, the thought of you with someone else, blah blah blah. When I didn't give in to his false repentance this time, he turned cold again.

"I have to leave for work," Matt said.

He grabbed his jacket and briefcase. The door slammed behind him, and everyone jumped. When I heard him peel out of the driveway, I set Jess into the playpen.

Am I having an affair? Ridiculous. He was the one carousing whenever he wanted without a thought of us. Most nights he came home smelling of alcohol and perfume. *He's the one screwing the whole town.*

"Oh, men like to have their fun, hon, but they always come home," Matt's mom said one day, ages ago, when I mentioned he wasn't home from work when she called after dinner.

I was stuck there all day, and now had another baby coming. *What am I going to do?* I was feeling trapped and completely stupid. Again. The last five years had been nothing but a revolving door of feeling trapped, and then feeling guilty for trapping myself.

I went into the kitchen to clean up the eggs. My back ached from being pressed against the counter. From the living room, Jen's voice rose to the piercing decibel only a toddler can reach. By the time I got into the living room, Julie had a handful of Jen's hair and wouldn't let go. Now everyone was crying, including me. I separated Julie's fingers from her sister's head, and Jen plunked her butt down with all the emotion of a child done wrong. Jess picked up her pacifier and used it to soothe herself as she held onto the soft yellow side of the playpen. I picked up Jen, put her on my hip, and turned to bring her into the kitchen for a snack.

Two steps later, a burning sensation tore through my abdomen. The pain went around my back and down my legs. I set Jen on the floor. I sat on the couch for a second, but then rushed to the bathroom. Cramping, I started a heavy period.

I cleaned up and got back out to the girls. Luckily, Jen hadn't gotten into anything, and Jess and Julie were still in the playpen. I didn't know what to think. *Was this just a late period?* I had them, but not this late. Or did the little breakfast scene cause a miscarriage? The carousel of feeling guilty, relieved, and angry kept me dizzy all day.

When Matt came home at seven-thirty, he said he grabbed a bite with a friend.

"I started my period," I said as he set his briefcase down.

He raised his eyebrows, nodded, and kissed the girls. For a while, he sat on the couch to watch TV. After Sonny and Cher, he took a shower and went to bed without a word to me.

After three days of Matt's silent treatment, he said, "I think it's time to visit the grandparents."

I smiled for the first time in four days. "How wonderful. We'll all have a great time for a couple of days away from work and home."

"Just you and the girls," he said.

"You're sending us away?"

"Yes." He talked so calmly that I wanted to punch him.

I grabbed Jess from the highchair and started for the bedroom. "We'll leave in the morning," I said at the threshold without turning around. I packed a few things for the girls and left before he got up the next morning.

Despite my distracted thoughts of how Matt was such an ass, the girls and I had a really good time. Matt's parents still lived near my parents, so it was nice to split the time to see them both. The girls loved all the attention from all their Grammas and Grampas.

The day we came home, Matt was waiting there for us. The girls ran to him on the couch. They giggled and hugged him as he blew raspberries into their necks.

Not saying a word to him, I went straight to the girls' room to unpack.

Matt came in and hugged me from behind. "I'm sorry, Beth. Can we start again? I wish we could just forget about the way we left things."

He had this wonderful, awful energy that made you forget everything else. Sinfully smooth charm paired with his looks made for a dangerous combination. Standing there with his arms around me, he swayed me back and forth and all my anger melted away. When his lips grazed the back of my neck, all I wanted to do was forget.

42 Years Ago

Chapter Twenty-Four

That's what I did. Forgot. I stretched my magic memory and blind eye for three years. Ignoring the frequent verbal and occasional physical abuse, I grew to enjoy his late nights out. The mistreatment was only directed at me, never the girls.

The girls' daily schedules: School, PTA, crafts, food, and their friends, became my escape. I also began regular lunches with my siblings, who still lived in the area.

Judy, my youngest sister, paced by the giant doors of The Ground Round. She was now nineteen and a grand beauty with long brown hair. When we hugged hello, Judy hung on a little longer than usual.

Inside, we followed the bubbly bleach blonde waitress to our booth. I noticed Judy fidgeting with her purse strings. On a closer inspection, I saw her coat wasn't buttoned properly, and she wore almost no make-up today, just a little lipstick.

"Thank you," I said when the waitress handed me the menu. As I looked over the lunch specials, I stole quick peeks at Judy. She looked pale and disheveled. Her hair was frizzy and thrown into a low ponytail. Had she been crying?

I ordered a cheeseburger and fries. Judy handed the menu to the waitress, "Same," she said without looking at the woman. The waitress left. I waited for Judy to tell me what was going on.

She wouldn't look at me. She sat there and looked at the kitschy decor or stared at the table, touching her fork and knife lightly.

It wasn't until her teardrops fell onto the table that I spoke up. "Judy, what's going on?"

With that, Judy broke into quiet sobs. She hid her face in her napkin and turned to the wall of our booth. "I'm such a fucking idiot," she said through the red linen cloth.

I slid out of my side of the booth and scooted in with her. I wrapped my arms around my sister and allowed her to sob until our food came.

Judy would not look at the waitress, she just said thank you quietly. She shoved a french fry in her mouth without a word, trying to look anywhere but at me.

"Seriously?" I asked in a low tone as I slid into my side of the booth. "After all that, you're not going to tell me what this is about? What happened in the last month that could have affected you so much?" I reached my hand out for hers. She pulled it back under the table. "I just talked to you on the phone last week."

Judy grabbed her napkin again and slid it back and forth between her hands.

"I haven't told you something that has been happening in my life for the last few months."

I had taken a bite of my burger and was now shoving a fry into my mouth. Judy looked at my face and then at the table again. "I have been having an affair with a married man," she whispered. I stopped chewing and my eyebrows went up.

"No way!" I said with a full mouth, then swallowed my bite. I knew the next words that would come out of Judy's mouth.

"And now I'm pregnant," Judy said and welled up.

Yup, I thought, but said, "Oh sweetheart, how long have you been seeing him?"

"Three months," Judy said, releasing tears again.

"Do I know him?"

There was a long pause.

"It's Matt," she whispered.

"Matt who?" As the words left my mouth, I realized. My Matt. My husband.

The silence at the table seemed to infect the whole restaurant. Or maybe I just couldn't hear anything over the sound of blood rushing in my ears.

"What?" Barreled out of my mouth. It was loud enough for the whole restaurant to hear. Now everything stopped, and all eyes were on us.

A little quieter now I went on, "What the hell are you telling me?" Standing now I went on, "You are having sex with my husband, and now you are pregnant! How can you tell me that?" I slammed down the giant red cloth napkin and fought the urge to leap over the table and strangle Judy. "Why would you choose to tell me here and now? Have you lost your mind?" I turned and walked out.

Judy called out behind me, "I haven't told him yet!"

I raced to my car. The engine roared before I was completely in the seat. As I peeled out of the parking spot, Judy was coming out of the big brown wooden doors. Her arms were outstretched, holding her hands together, begging me to stop. I didn't. I also didn't run her over, so there was some control on my part.

Driving around town on autopilot, I found myself sitting in the car with the big blue CARLTON HOTEL sign staring me in the face. I let out a primal scream as I slammed my hands on the steering wheel over and over.

I forced myself across the parking lot and into the hotel where my husband worked. Steam swirled in my head, jumbling my thoughts together.

I passed the girl at the front desk and rounded the corner. I walked down the hall and right into Matt's office. He sat at his meticulously arranged desk with the telephone to his ear.

As soon as he saw me, he stood. "I'll have to call you back," he said to the person on the line. I walked in, shut the door, and locked it.

I waited a few heartbeats before I turned, then took a deep breath and faced him.

"Beth, you're a mess. Is everything okay?" he asked. "Is there something wrong with the girls?"

"No, the girls are fine. I just got some upsetting news and needed to tell you."

"Okay," he said, "sit down."

I sat in one of two plush orange leather chairs in the corner of his office near the window. He sat in the other one.

We mirrored each other, both on the edge of the chair leaning forward, elbows on our knees, silent. He was looking at me and I was looking at my hands. After all the arguments I had with him in my head on my drive, what came out was simple.

I looked him in the eyes and said, "Judy's pregnant."

It took less than a second for my phrase to sink in. First, I watched as he realized he was in trouble, and then I saw Matt realize I knew all the details.

He leaned back in his chair and folded his hands on his chest. "Well," he said. "That's unfortunate."

"Unfortunate?" I seethed, even though his callousness shouldn't surprise me by this time in our marriage.

He stood from the brightly colored seat and walked to the middle of the room. His hand rubbed his forehead down to his chin. "Yes, unfortunate."

"You're unbelievable," I said and walked towards him. "Do you even care for either of us?"

"I don't know, hon, you Shelby girls just give it up so quick." He grabbed me around the waist with one hand and the other hand went between my legs.

"You must take after the mother that abandoned you to slut it up all over New England."

He jammed his face between my chin and shoulder and started kissing my neck. I pushed him back, but his grasp was too tight. As I struggled, he squeezed harder. I did the only thing I could. My knee came up and brought him to all fours in an instant.

"Fuck you, Matt," I yelled down at him. With him down on the floor, I sent my foot to his ribs. He gave a satisfying groan. "Fuck you."

As I put my hand on the door to leave, I heard Matt, he groaned from the floor with his finger pointed at me.

"You just wait," he coughed, "until I get home."

I turned to him and held up both hands with my middle fingers extended and circled them in the air. Then, grabbing the door handle, I shouted, "You will never touch me again!"

As I passed the front desk girl, I stopped and put both hands on the counter. "Don't fool yourself, sweetie. He's a cheater and an abuser." I flicked a piece of shirt at her that Matt ripped in our scuffle.

She nodded to me slowly with wide eyes, as one does to a crazy person. I rushed out of the hotel towards my car.

As I dug in my purse for keys, a loud crash came from the intersection. I craned my neck to see a powder blue VW Bug had smashed into a Cadillac. I knew that VW Bug.

"Judy," I said in a desperate whisper as I sprinted across the blacktop straight into the street. At that moment, Judy was not the sister bitch that wronged me. She was simply my sister, and she may be hurt.

I could see that Judy crashed her Bug head-on into the Caddy's driver's side. The force of the blow looked to have spun the other car 180 degrees. My sister's mass of hair was strewn across the steering wheel. I opened her door and sat Judy back on the seat. Blood covered most of her face. She came around after I called her name a couple of times.

Judy held her arm tight to her body. "Sorry," she said and passed out again.

Tears filled my eyes. Judy had always been damaged. She spent her youngest childhood years in an orphanage and left when she should have been loved.

Matt's the real villain here, I tried to remind myself. My sister was as young and naïve as I had been when Matt seduced me. I moved Judy's hair off her face and held her hand as I waited for the emergency vehicles.

At the hospital, the green waiting room chairs were filled with moms with their coughing kids, an elderly couple holding hands, and men pacing back and forth. I waited there until Dad brought Mom and my girls. When I told them about the accident (not the pregnancy), my mom lost all breath and grabbed my dad's arm for stability.

At six p.m. the doctor came out, "Judy has two broken ribs, a broken right arm, and has dislocated her left hip." And then, before I could stop him, "The baby was lost, and Miss Shelby's uterus had extensive damage. She likely can never have another pregnancy."

My mother and father stood there open-mouthed. They looked at me because I didn't seem surprised. I thanked the doctor and then walked my parents to the waiting room row of chairs.

"I only found out she was pregnant today. She told me at lunch."

"Who is the father?" they asked.

I thought about it for a second, and then spared them the drama for now. "She wouldn't tell me."

I asked to see Judy first. I pushed open the solid wood hospital door and saw my sister lying there. She stared at the ceiling. I could see the wet streaks of tears that connected the corner of her eye with her hairline.

When Judy saw me, she turned towards the window. "Not now Beth. I know I fucked up."

"That mouth, my goodness?" I said. I sat next to her and stroked her hair.

Judy turned with knitted brows. "You aren't mad at me?"

"Oh, I'm pissed, but you're my sister." I sat on the edge of the bed and placed my hand on Judy's shoulder. "All night I've been going back and forth between 'How could she do this,' and 'How could Matt do this?' Talking about it now, I guess I'm a little more pissed than I thought." I pressed harder on Judy's shoulder.

"Beth, you're hurting me."

I didn't let up. In fact, I leaned in. "Tell Mom and Dad what you want. I didn't tell them I knew who the father was. I'll try to forgive you, but it will take time." I gave one final push to Judy's damaged arm and left the room.

I asked my parents to take the girls home. "Matt has started happy hour early. Please don't let him drive the kids home. I'll be back later." I thanked and kissed them both and walked out of the hospital.

Chapter Twenty-Five

My brain flip-flopped between compassion and anger too many times today. *I need a drink.*

I found myself at a bar near the hospital. Halfway into my Tom Collins, a mustached Romeo sidled up beside me.

"Hey, gorgeous. Where have you been all my life?" Seriously, he said that. I laughed in his face, then apologized. "I'm Sam, and I'm a Libra."

I let him tell me his life story. Not that I could have stopped him. "Next round's on me," he said, pointing to the bartender to bring another Tom Collins for me and a beer for him.

After I drained my second drink, he asked, "Want to dance?" I didn't answer but stood and started walking to the dance floor. The band was playing a song I didn't recognize, but it was easy to move to. We danced closer and closer. He leaned in to kiss me. At that moment, I made a conscious decision to let him.

The only word I said to this person was "Sorry" earlier when I laughed at him. He didn't know my name, or that I had three kids. Maybe he caught the wedding ring, but it was obvious he didn't care. At that moment, neither did I.

He led me off the dance floor, around the corner, and down the hall to the bathroom. He shut and locked the bathroom door and backed me up against the wall. I had never done anything like this, although I gave no resistance.

I wanted to feel like anyone but myself tonight. Pouring into this stranger, I forgot about all the hate that had been growing inside. Unbuckling his belt and dropping his jeans, I pushed him onto the toilet. I lifted my skirt and positioned myself on him. I shut my eyes and became free of everyone that hurt me.

After I reached my peak, I rose and straightened my clothes. I unlocked the door and left him there, unsatisfied, still not having said more than one word to him. I went to pick up the girls from my parent's house, but in the end, decided we should all sleep there.

I packed a few things while Matt was at work the next day and left that apartment forever.

I got one day with Mom and Dad to pretend to be just visiting. Two days after the crash, Judy came home to find me in her house with my kids.

The next day, Judy quit her job over the phone. In the newspaper, there was a nanny job with live-in quarters in Boston. With only a phone interview, she was hired. She carried just one suitcase when my dad drove her there three days later, cracked ribs and all.

A few days after that, I told my parents about Matt's abuse and that I wasn't going back. They welcomed us with open arms. It took me a while to get up the nerve to tell Matt that this wasn't just a visit.

The divorce was messy and living with my parents was uncomfortable. Most nights after everyone was asleep, I would put my hair up, slide my lipstick on, and head out to a bar and find another Romeo. Never the same bar, never the same guy, never a word. The music was always loud and overcame the thoughts in my head. The disconnect was comforting and the flight from who I was, was necessary. It didn't take long though and even those nights became hollow.

My circling thoughts like *How could I let things get like this,* and *I should have never married him,* kept crushing me into bed with covers over my head. Sometimes Mom brought me food. Sometimes I ate. The girls would lie with me. I had no words for them.

After two weeks in bed, my mom came into my room and sat on the chair in the corner. She was quiet for a long time and then said, "You know, if you stay in bed," she paused, "he wins." I peeped out from under the blanket and saw her smirk and walk out.

A wail escaped me, while my hands and feet thumped on the bed again and again like a child who didn't want to take a bath. The numbness in my body turned hot. "I'm lost in my missteps. I'm a twenty-five-year-old failure," I called out.

"How could you be a failure?" she asked, poking her head back into the room. "Three precious girls wait for you in the living room, filling their days with television and Grammy's cookies until you are ready."

I turned and brought the covers over my head again. This time, I planned instead of wallowing. I plotted the next steps of my life.

The next morning, I rose from my blanket cocoon and took a shower. After I put on clean clothes and braided my damp hair into two neat plaits, I sat on a kitchen chair. Mom was drying the breakfast dishes.

"I need a job," I said.

"Popsy's needs a waitress. You could start there," she said without hesitation. She knew this was coming. She knew me. Mom put the clean glass in the cabinet and turned around. "I would watch the girls whenever you needed."

I took the job as a waitress. In time, I was able to afford a small two-bedroom apartment in town. It was above the hardware store where my first boyfriend, Luke, used to work. Almost every day I was reminded of my secret sweet sixteen romance with my brother's best friend. My mind wandered sometimes, thinking of our candy kisses in the storeroom.

37 Years Ago

Chapter Twenty-Six

Time passed, and Matt took the girls now and then. They went to the park or a movie. He also came to see me now and then and we would have passionate, needful sex. It seemed easy to forget the bad stuff when it felt so far away. Fool.

One night, Matt and I fell asleep before I could tell him to leave. In the morning, Jess came bounding into the bedroom, with Julie screaming after her. They both jumped into the bed where Matt and I were asleep. Pulling a hairbrush back and forth, one yelled, "I had it first!" then the other, "NO! I did!"

Matt jumped up out of the bed, grabbed the hairbrush, and dragged Julie off the bed by her arm. I launched myself towards him. He dropped the hairbrush only to grab a whole fist full of my long brown hair.

"Everybody shut up," he shouted as he stood there in his underwear, still holding Julie and my tresses.

The girls were shocked into silence. I writhed on the floor, wildly grabbing at his hand, trying to detach fingers from my head of hair. He let us go, and I lay there, stunned at the scene.

I recovered and rose to stand between him and the girls. I grabbed his clothes from the chair and threw them at him.

"Get out!" I screamed in a voice that didn't seem like my own.

I ran to Julie on the floor holding her upper arm. It already started to bruise. Jess was at my leg. I picked her up onto my hip.

I said to Matt, "If you ever come near us again, I will call the police."

"How will you get the child support?" he asked with a bastard of a smile.

I got a hold of myself as my confidence rose. "Mail it," I said with a stone cold face.

He stooped down to pick up his clothes. "Come on, sweetie." He took one step toward us.

"Get. Out," I said, throwing his shoes at him to drive my point home. "Or I will call the police right now." As he dodged the shoes, he tried to figure out if I was bluffing.

"Fine!" Throwing his free hand into the air. "Happy to!" Bending down to grab his shoes, he said, "The only good thing about having this family was that it kept me out of Vietnam! You can all kiss my ass." He flipped me off and stormed out.

Jen came down the hall, "Daddy?" she said in my doorway.

He walked right past her without a word. She watched him walk out the bedroom door, down the hall, and out the front door wearing only his underwear, holding his clothes and shoes bundled in his arms.

Jen rushed to Julie, who was still sniffling. I set Jess on the floor. Drained of all energy, I sunk to the floor, supported by the bed. The girls piled on top of me. We cried, and I apologized over and over. I patted their hair and held their heads in my hands.

Two hours passed before Julie stirred. Jen's arms had been around her the whole time. They just lay there together like twins in the womb. Jess was asleep on my thigh. I hadn't dared to move this whole time, hoping somehow my presence would heal them from the trauma that had transpired.

I felt Julie's finger tap my chest. "Pancakes," she said. "We need pancakes." Waking at the sound of the sweet cakes, the other girls assured me this was true, so we went to the kitchen.

I mixed up some pancake batter and tried to talk about anything but their father. I turned the radio up and soon we were dancing and chewing on syrupy discs of happiness.

Chapter Twenty-Seven

My kitchen table was littered with past-due notices. Matt had sent no child support for over three months. He never even called for the girls. After one month, his phone stopped working. I called Laura and my in-laws. If they knew where he was, they weren't telling me. When I asked the police to investigate it, they said he moved from his apartment and quit his job. There was no forwarding address. He was just gone, like my biological father long ago.

Tears rolled down my face. *If I could have just kept my mouth shut, or my legs, I wouldn't be in this position.*

Letting that thought wash over me, I thought of the last day I saw Matt. I thought of Julie sobbing on the floor, her arm bruised from his grip. I looked into that future with Matt getting more and more violent to us all.

With my hands pulling at the roots of my hair, I tried to shake the image from my brain. I was on my feet now, pacing my small kitchen. *That future will never happen.*

Back and forth, I walked from one kitchen wall to the other. Every time, passing years of family photos hung on the wall. My eyes landed on Matt's fake smile in our last photo shoot.

I grabbed the photo off the wall and shook it like I wished I could shake Matt. *I hate you. How could you? How could you?*

I was whispering. Tears wet my cheeks and fell onto the glass of the frame. I wanted to throw it. Break the glass and tear his face into a million pieces. But that might wake the girls.

And? I blinked. *So what if the girls heard?*

I chucked the picture and frame to the floor. I used my fuzzy slipper to stomp Matt's face again and again. Getting down to my knees, I swished the broken glass away. I picked up the photo and tore it into hundreds of little pieces. Every tear of the photo freed me more.

I sat there laughing on the kitchen floor. Sitting in a pile of broken glass and little photo bits. I rested my arm and head on the seat of the chair next to me, breathing easy for the first time in months; maybe years.

After half an hour, I stood. The stack of bills still piled on the table wasn't as scary this time. I drummed my fingers on my top lip. If I couldn't make enough at my job, I needed a new job. The answer was so easy that I marveled I hadn't thought of it before.

Every day I scoured the want-ads before my shift at the diner. The fear of moving back to my parents gripped my heart after two weeks of no luck. *Is there anything that would pay enough that would allow us to stay in our apartment?* I sent up a silent prayer to whatever was there for help.

The very next day, there it was. The job I left to have Julie was open again. I sat with my hand covering my open mouth. Over ten years later, the same dentist's office was looking for a receptionist.

After my shift, I drove over to the office. They hired me on the spot. It only took a little time to adjust to the new systems. The flow of work was familiar, and I fell back into a routine. No more getting drinks spilled on me or my butt slapped. No more counting tips and hoping that I could buy bread and milk and still have enough for the electricity. Money was still tight, but we could stay in our apartment.

Chapter Twenty-Eight

The song from my clock radio woke me up at six in the morning. I grabbed a cup of coffee at Mom and Dad's when I dropped the girls off. Mom took the girls to and from school. I left the dentist's office at five thirty and picked them up at six in the evening. That was the schedule Monday through Thursday. The dentist's office was always closed for a long weekend.

On Friday, I took the girls to school and picked them up. I used this day off to catch up on housework, see friends, or go shopping.

The weekends were all about the girls. Us against the world. In winter, we made snowmen and had snowball fights in the park or cuddled up close with books under a blanket fort. In summer, we had camping or beach days; we were forever tanned, and mosquito bitten.

Late one night, I sat finishing a library book when a thought hit me.

"Matt was the reason Matt left, not me. Matt was the reason Matt was an ass, not me. I'm the reason we are safe, happy, and cozy here in our apartment. Just us. Just perfect."

When I realized I had been talking out loud, I thanked the empty room for listening, put down my book, and went to bed.

As they got older, the girls' friends would always come along on our outings. Everyone would pile into the back seat on top of one another. I bought a Polaroid instant camera and started filling the walls with pictures of our adventures.

35 Years Ago

Chapter Twenty-Nine

The summer when Julie was twelve, we were on the beach enjoying the waves together. Dripping wet and walking to our beach towels, I heard someone call my name.

"Beth," the person said, "is that you?"

"Sara Jane?" I said before I even turned around. "How are you?" I asked, ready to throw my arms around her.

I stopped mid-reach, seeing my dripping arms and her dry blouse. I smiled and drew my arms back to my chest, but she threw her arms around me. When we released each other, I saw I had soaked through her white blouse, revealing her daisy covered lavender bikini top. "Nice suit," I laughed.

"Thanks!" she said, smiling at me and pulling at her shirt a bit to get some air between the top and her skin. Then, looking over my shoulder, she asked, "Are these your girls?"

"Yes!" I beamed. "This is Julie, Jen, and Jess. We come here all the time. What are you doing here?"

"I'm visiting my parents," Sara Jane said as she pointed up the beach. "My mom rents a cottage here every year so we can have a family reunion." Her parents waved at us from their sun chairs.

"It is so good to see you!" she continued. "We were just about to leave. Can you visit us sometime this week? My husband and I just got here. We'll be here until next Sunday."

"Sounds great! I'd love to catch up."

"What about tomorrow? We are having a barbecue at the cottage. You and the girls could come."

I looked at the girls, who were looking at me with eyes full of hope. Jen was bouncing with clutched together pleading hands. "It looks like we are all in agreement. What time, where, and, of course, what should I bring?" I asked.

"Do you see that blue house down the street?" She pointed.

"The one with two stories and white shutters?"

"That's the one. Be there around eleven tomorrow." Thinking aloud as she scratched her head, she continued. "Hmm, what can you bring?" She dropped her hand from her head and tapped on her chin. "I know!" she said, pointing at the girls. "Do any of you know how to make chocolate chip cookies?"

Jess hugged Julie's waist and muffled a squeal into her side. "You bet. We know a great recipe," Julie assured Sarah Jane.

"Oh good, then that is your job." Sara Jane smiled back at me and grabbed my hands. "I can't wait to see you."

We hugged again and went back to our separate spots on the beach.

At our beach towels, the girls begged to go home right away and start the cookies. We patted ourselves dry with sandy towels and piled into our steamy car for the fifteen-minute drive home.

At home, the girls and I changed and met in the kitchen. They knew the drill. Julie measured the ingredients and Jess poured them into the bowl. Jen was in control of the mixer. I supervised and protected the chocolate chips. When everything was mixed, I scooped the batter out onto the sheet pans and gave the girls the bowl to lick clean. Of course, we had to quality test them when they were done.

With the cookies cooling, the girls went to watch some television. I went to choose what I would wear tomorrow. It was between my olive-green jumpsuit and my yellow floor-length dress with little orange flowers. The dress won out in the end; it may keep me cooler. Orange hoop earrings and orange bangles completed my look.

In the morning, I tied my hair up in a high ponytail and brushed blue eye shadow across my lids. I spread black mascara on my lashes and finished off with blush and clear lip gloss. I looked in the mirror, plucked a few stray eyebrow hairs, then I was satisfied.

At ten-thirty, we boxed up the cookies, grabbed the camera, and headed to the car. Just before we left, I grabbed our swimsuits and towels. Even if we hated being at the barbecue, maybe we could stop at the lake for a bit.

Sarah Jane saw us right away and welcomed us in. She ushered us over to her parents. Jess handed the cookies to Sarah Jane's dad.

"Did you make these?" he asked.

"We all did," she said sheepishly, looking down at her shoes.

Sarah Jane's father gave us a big toothy grin and said, "Well, chocolate chip cookies are my favorite, and *I* won't wait to have one." He opened the box and munched one right then and there. "How about you?"

He held the container out to Jen and the girls. They giggled and grabbed one, too. From then on, I knew we wouldn't need to escape to the beach.

Chatting here and there throughout the house, Sarah Jane's aunts, uncles, and cousins were all around. The girls grabbed the camera. They quickly found some kids their age and were off to have amazing adventures.

Sarah Jane pulled me aside on the quieter side of the yard with a couple of red lawn chairs. As I sat with her, I was transported to a simpler time. We just seemed like teens again, sitting around, catching up on our summer vacation. Except it had been over ten years and we lived completely different lives.

We reviewed what we already knew. She went to college to get her teaching degree. I got preggers and married Matt. Then the newer stuff came out. She graduated and went to a small-town school to teach second grade. She met Rob, a geography teacher at the high school, a year after moving there and married a year after that. I had two more girls after Julie and divorced Matt.

When Sarah-Jane had been in her small town for about a year, she wandered into the little community church and had been going ever since. We grew up going to church on Sundays, but I was out of that scene as soon as possible.

"Don't think I'm crazy, but do you believe in God?" Sarah Jane asked.

"God never crosses my mind." I felt no reason to veil the truth.

"I do now. I even believe that Jesus was His son." She pulled out a small book from her back pocket. *The New Testament and Psalms* were written in gold on the front of the fake green leather. She told me I could have it in case I ever wanted to read about Jesus's life.

"Thanks," I said, slipping it into my purse to be nice, though now a little uncomfortable. Thankfully, she sensed this and changed the subject.

"Do you keep in touch with anyone we used to hang out with?" she asked, sitting back on the lounge part of the chair.

"Not really. Just Laura. She lives in Minnesota now with her husband. They have twin baby boys that just turned two. Cuties." I pulled a picture out of my wallet. She cooed at it and handed it back. "Most people moved away after high school. I did too but came back after the divorce." My voice trailed off.

A child's wail came from the driveway. I knew it was Jess before all three girls popped out from behind the side of the house.

"What happened?" I asked as she ran to me.

"I hurt my arm," she said with eyes about to burst again. She shoved her scraped arm under my nose with her bottom lip sticking out as far as possible. There were three red scratches, but no flowing blood.

Julie and Jen were nodding their heads. "She tripped on the grass near the driveway." Julie told us.

I brought my lips to Jess's forehead.

Sarah Jane jumped up in theatrical horror with her hands in front of her mouth. "Do you need an ambulance?"

"I don't think so," Jess said and wiped her wet cheeks with the back of her good arm.

"Do you think you could make it through if you had a little ice cream?" Jess's pout went straight to a smile.

Sarah Jane popped into the house and came out with ice cream for all the kids. Julie's and Jen's faces lit up. "Thanks!" all three girls said in unison.

Sarah Jane and I talked a bit more, and she introduced me to many extended family members. At about six thirty, Sarah Jane and I snapped what is now known as a selfie with the Polaroid, then the girls and I piled into the car. There were no more cookies.

Instead, my container was filled with chicken and potato salad leftovers to eat for lunch this week.

At home, just before I went to sleep, I grabbed Sarah Jane's bible. I thumbed through it under my covers, propped up on my pillows. I looked at the last section, which I assumed was the end of Jesus' life. I was wrong. It was very odd with seals and scrolls, real end-of-the-world stuff. *To each their own*, I thought and tossed it in my side table drawer.

33 Years Ago

Chapter Thirty

On the first Saturday in September, Happy Birthday Julie and Jen was written on the big cake from Peggy's bakery. A big fifteen and fourteen were next to each girl's name. My parents let me have the party at their place and all the girls' friends were there.

I clicked the shutter button on my camera as Julie and Jen blew out the candles. I grabbed the picture from the slot to give it the *development wave.* That is what the girls called my unnecessary action of whipping the Polaroid photo back and forth.

When Julie was thirteen, she told me she kissed a boy. When Jen was thirteen, she told me she kissed a girl. What on earth would happen next year when Jess was thirteen? I decided not to restrict my girls' dating. Opting instead to make sure they know all the pitfalls and damaging things that came along with knowing someone beyond friendship. We talked honestly about men, women, sex, dating, STDs, birth control, abuse, and any other thing that could happen during a romantic relationship.

I was in unfamiliar territory with Jen but deciding that all relationships have the same basic need for love and respect, I did my best with everything else. I stressed a lesson I learned: attraction is not a relationship. Feeling that feverish need to kiss, and more, with someone, is not love. It's a normal need, but love is something deeper where you want to be with them because you inspire each other to be better.

I also called and talked with Patty and Betty. A lot. When they came out to me years ago, I enfolded them both in my arms and told them I love them no matter what. Patty was proud of Jen when she came out at such a young age, but nervous about the teasing and abuse she might have to endure. She set up a weekly call with all the girls, but secretly she called to give Jen advice learned from experience.

Because I started open communication early with Julie, it extended even younger with Jen and Jess, because we would talk openly at the dinner table, on the couch, wherever, and whenever they needed. I was honored when they trusted me enough to bring any problem or question, and proud that my home was a haven for them to be free and who they were. That was soon followed by their friends.

I was simply known as "Ma" by most of the kids in the town. Life was a revolving door of teens. Sleepovers littered my living room with girls most weekends. I always made sure there was popcorn, chips, sodas, and popsicles. I captured every minute with my instant camera.

Today's birthday party reminded me we had been doing things on our own for quite a while now. I had no loneliness or yearning for a partner. Maybe I would have enjoyed some help on those late nights when certain urges would arise, but they were fleeting.

Chapter Thirty-One

As it does, life brings you along in crazy ways.

Thursday, September 18, started like any other Thursday. I got us ready and out the door. After I talked with Mom and Dad for a minute over a cup of coffee, I kissed the girls and headed to work.

After lunch, the office door chimes rang. Sitting at my desk, I looked up with a smile, ready to greet the next patient. "Good aft-" I trailed off. My eyes squinted and my head tilted. My legs automatically tightened and brought me to standing.

He chatted and laughed casually as he walked in with a gray-haired woman. His brown hair was long enough to touch his shoulders, his almost golden eyes were bright as ever, and his electric smile shot through me from head to toe. Luke.

He stopped too when he saw me. Still smiling, he cocked his head. "Beth?" he said and turned to the markedly shorter gray-haired woman. She was smiling too because she knew what was going on.

He wasn't on the patient list. The next patient was Elsa Desmond, a new patient in for tooth pain.

My smile came back to me. "Luke? Mrs. Marcome?" blinking my brain back to the present.

"It's Mrs. Desmond, dear," she said, as I walked out from behind the desk, never taking my eyes off them.

"How are you? What are you doing here?" I asked as I took her hand. I looked from Elsa to Luke and back again.

"Mom asked me to drive her here," Luke said, smiling and staring at me. "She is coming in to see Dr. Massie."

"Of course," I brought my hand to my forehead and shook off the embarrassment. *Of course, she was there to see the dentist.* "It's just amazing that you came here. It's such a surprise to see you. My mother told me you moved to Russell ages ago."

"I bumped into your mother last year. She told me you were working here," Elsa said with a wry smile. "I found myself in need of a dentist and thought I'd try Dr. Massie again. He was always a good dentist when I lived in town."

"What a sneak," Luke laughed out the words. "You knew Beth might be here this whole time?"

"I thought, if she was still here, it would be nice for you two to see one another again," Elsa said with a smirk and a shoulder shrug. "If not, no harm done."

"Please, Mrs. Mar-, um, Desmond, please sit down and tell me how you are." I guided her to the waiting room chairs.

"Well, dear, as you know, Luke went off to the Army and not too long after that, I moved to Russell. After a few years there, I met a wonderful man and remarried," she said and then turned to Luke. "Luke stayed in the Army for a bit. They sent him to Vietnam. He was wounded and came home." My eyes darted to Luke and looked him over.

"I'm fine." He held up his hand. His voice, deeper than when he was a teen, gave me chills. "I caught a bullet in the thigh. I just have a slight limp now," he said as he patted his left leg.

"Oh, I'm glad you are fine now. Sorry you had to go through that."

"I'm just happy to be alive," he said with his classic velvet smile. I hoped my eyes didn't betray how much I wanted to melt into the chairs.

Donna, the dental nurse, came out and called for Mrs. Desmond. "I'll see you two soon. Sit and catch up a bit." Elsa patted Luke on the leg and started down the hall.

"Isn't she something?" Luke said as he watched her walk away. "Paul, the man she married, is great. They asked for my blessing after I got back. When I saw how happy they were, I couldn't say no," he said, still looking at the hall. Then, turning to me, he said, "He owns a grocery store in Russell. That's where they met."

"How nice for them both. I'm happy to see her doing so well." Folding my jittery hands together, I asked, "What about you? Work? Family?"

He gave a little chuckle. "It turns out I was great with wires and the Army trained me as an electrician. When I came back from Vietnam, I got a job with Precision Electric in Huntington and have worked there ever since. As for my family, I just have Mom and Paul."

Color rushed to my cheeks when he asked me the same questions. "Well, I was married to Matt Bonnet, but we divorced." *How much should I go into here?* I thought. "I have 3 lovely girls. We rent the apartment above the hardware shop you worked at as a teen."

"No kidding?" He said with a half laugh. "Wow, three girls. That's amazing."

The door chimes jingled, signaling another patient. Breaking my gaze, I turned to her. "Good afternoon, Miss Reynolds. Please have a seat. Stephanie will be right out for you." Turning to Luke, "I'm sorry, you'll have to excuse me."

"Of course, do what you need to. I'll be here."

I walked behind the desk to check off Miss Reynolds' name. I told Stephanie Miss Reynolds was here, and walked as calmly as I could to the restroom. Thankful of being out of the eyesight of anyone, I leaned against the wall with my hand over my mouth and slid down to the floor. I let out my silent scream and then composed myself.

I walked back to my desk and saw a teen sitting in one of the blue waiting room chairs. "Hi Ginny," I said with a smile. "Joanne will be out in just a moment."

"Thanks," Ginny said back and gave me a big smile that revealed a mouth full of braces.

Looking out from behind my desk, I searched the room for Luke. He was gone. *Elsa was still here. Where did he go?*

"The man that was here said he was going out for some air," Ginny told me.

"Thanks, honey," I said and sat back down in my chair to look at the schedule. Ginny was the last patient today. I was just about to step out back again when Luke came in and walked over to the desk.

"Is there any way we can see each other again? My mom is just about finished, and I would really like to do some more catching up." I gave a side glance to Ginny, who smiled with wide eyes, nodding her head.

I gathered all the calm I could muster. "Sure, I'm off Fridays, Saturdays, and Sundays. The girls are in school on Fridays until three. Maybe next week?"

"Do you have any plans for lunch tomorrow? I don't work on Fridays either."

Stopped short at the thought of seeing him again so soon, all I could manage was, "That would work."

"How about lunch at Popsy's for old times' sake? Maybe about eleven?"

"Perfect."

"I'll see you there," he said as Elsa came through the door into the waiting room.

"Have a good day, dear. It was lovely to see you," Elsa said with the same smile as her son.

The door closed behind them, and all my strength left me. I sat back in my chair and put my hands on my head. I hadn't even noticed when Ginny got called in.

Mrs. Reynolds left, and Stephanie walked over to my desk. She leaned on the counter. "Who was that?" Her ear-to-ear grin said *Dish!*

"Just an old friend," I said without looking up as I gathered some papers on my desk. "We're having lunch tomorrow to catch up." I could feel her eyes still on me. "Don't worry," I said with a smile, "I'll tell you everything on Monday." She seemed satisfied with that and went about cleaning her tools so she could go home to her family.

When Ginny left, I closed the office. Safely in my car, alone, I couldn't help letting out a loud satisfying shout. At Mom's I said, "You will never believe who came in today." She listened to the entire story without blinking. When I asked her to pick up the girls from school tomorrow, she was happy to.

Chapter Thirty-Two

Sitting across from Luke was surreal. His paisley shirt, open at the neck, was tucked into his bell bottom jeans. It looked great under his brown leather bomber jacket.

We began with, "How are you?", "Oh fine, thanks, and you?" like it was any old person you would have met on the street. Taking my arms out of my coat and shoving it down in the seat behind me, I sat on my hands so he wouldn't see them shaking.

A new waitress at Popsy's came up to take our order. Only about seventeen, she was a scrawny thing with glasses. Her strawberry hair was pulled tight on the top of her head.

"What can I get you?" she asked, her pencil at the ready, staring at me in fear of getting my order wrong.

Seeing her tension, I ordered a simple cheeseburger with fries and a Coke. Looking relieved, she turned to Luke, her eyebrows raised to her hairline. "I'll have the same, please," he said.

She let out her breath, now confident she could get the order to the table. "Right away!" she said and shuffled off.

"Boy, she looked terrified." Luke said, "Good idea to keep your order easy."

"I worked here a while after the divorce. I know how she feels."

When I mentioned the divorce, Luke asked more about it. I relaxed my shoulders a bit and told him all about the nightmare that was Matt. I could see fire in his eyes as I told him about the last time I saw Matt.

"Men like that should be drawn and quartered," he said, I didn't disagree.

He told me about the nightmare that was Vietnam. The bullet he caught in the hip was gone, but it left him with a slight limp and pain on rainy days. Luke never had children, but he was married for three years.

His wife, Daily, was a nurse. Three months after their wedding day she found out she had breast cancer. She died just days after Christmas, three years ago. The hurt shone in his eyes, but it was an old wound. My heart broke for him, and I slipped one hand from under my thighs to reach across the table to his forearm.

"It was like dragging myself up from Hell to grieve for her. Being close enough to my mom to help from time to time, like yesterday, helped me to remember there are still loved ones here on earth for me."

The waitress came up to the table with our food; the plates shaking on her tray held up by her palm and shoulder. "Will you need anything else?" she asked with eyes that said *please don't.* Luke and I shook our heads, and she ran off to do her other duties.

After our first few quiet bites, Luke blurted, "Look, Beth, I want to say I'm sorry about how I made things go all those years ago. I think of how things went from time to time, and it has been a great regret of mine."

I couldn't bring my eyes to him right away. I swallowed the bite of burger, almost choking on it, and slowly looked up. "I regret how I acted too," I breathed. "We were just kids though, we didn't know anything, but thought we knew everything." I rolled my eyes and smiled. "I hold nothing against you, and I hope you forgive me for my part."

"Of course." He ran his hand through his hair and sat back against the booth. After a pause, he said, "These fries are still great, aren't they? Just like I remember."

"Yes," I said. "The girls and I come here from time to time. It's fun to take them places I went when I was a kid."

We chatted more about the town and the fall weather as we ate. When we were done, he looked at his watch. "Wow, it's one-thirty. Don't you have to pick up the kids?"

"I asked my mom to do that. I wanted to be able to chat without watching the clock. I'm glad I did. I hardly noticed the time going by."

"Seeing as you don't have to rush off, would you like to take a walk?"

I slipped my arms back into my coat and stood. "Perfect idea."

We stepped out into the cool, sunny day and I turned in the opposite direction from my apartment. The crisp air had that hint of leaves that comes with New England autumns. We walked down Main Street and into the park. It was familiar and awkward at the same time.

"What are your girls like?" he asked.

I beamed. "Well, Julie is fifteen, quiet and loving. She is always willing to help anyone. She gets dragged into a lot of trouble with Jen. Jen is a riot and so outspoken. Man, the antics that girl comes up with at fourteen. If she isn't damaged or arrested by graduation, I'll be happy." Laughing, I continued. "Jess is a spitfire in glasses. When she sets her mind on something, watch out. She's taking dance lessons and insists she will be a prima ballerina one day." I made a terrible impression of a pirouette.

"You look amazing when you talk about them." Luke stopped and stood near a bench.

Color came to my cheeks, and I scrunched my nose. "Really?"

"Oh ya, I can really see the love and pride you have for them. Your eyes shine." He flashed that thought-crushing smile and looked at the ground. "It's beautiful."

He's going to be trouble. I turned and looked at the trees' changing leaves.

I sat on a bench, but Luke stood for a moment. When he sat down, it was closer to me than he needed. I turned to look at him and then turned my eyes back to my lap.

"It is really fun to get to know you again," I said.

"Are you kidding? This has been a blast. Can I see you again?" He spoke with the ease of someone not bothered by anything.

My heart stopped.

"I would really like that." My brain was trying everything possible not to let me say the next words, but I opened my mouth, and they came out. "But I want to be upfront with you. I don't want anything romantic in my life right now. The girls and I are in a good place," I said, looking him in the eyes.

"I completely understand. I'm just hoping to get to know you again," he said and popped off the bench. He reached out his hand to help me up. I took it and almost caught fire. I put my head down so my hair could hopefully cover my schoolgirl grin. *I'm such a hypocrite.*

I let him hold my hand as we walked for a while. When we got back to Popsy's, we said goodbye with numbers exchanged and a promise to call to set up plans for Friday. He got in his car and drove off and I walked the block and a half to my apartment.

In the safety of my empty house, I let out another of those satisfying screams and threw in a run-in-place for good measure.

We got together the next Friday, and the Friday after that. It was now a regular thing. He never pushed me to get closer, and he never made a move on me. We talked about everything under the sun on those Fridays.

One week as Luke and I were quietly eating our meatloaf specials at Popsy's, he asked, "What do you think about God?"

"I honestly don't know. Sarah Jane gave me a New Testament a couple of years ago. I read the Revelation, and it freaked me out."

He took a deep breath and then said, "I've been going to a little church in my town since Daily died," he said. "I have come to believe deeply in God and Jesus."

The orange carrot pile on my plate became very interesting and decidedly needed my attention.

"I agree Revelation is weird," he said. "But some of the other books are clearer. That is what the Bible is; a book of books," he said.

"Maybe I should give it another try."

"Start with one of the gospels this time. They are the books where four different people tell of the life of Jesus. They are the ones called Matthew, Mark, John, and," he smiled, "Luke."

Raising an eyebrow, I smiled at him. "Well then, that settles it. I'll try to read that this week. I still have the little bible in my side table. I'll pull it out tonight.

He nodded and then changed the subject, telling me about an interesting call he went out on to run wires into someone's garage. The client kept calling it a "Mood Room." Lots of different couches, a bed, and a disco ball. His humorous details pulled me out of my slight uncomfortableness from the God conversation.

As I pulled on my night shirt that evening, I glanced at the side table and remembered the bible in my drawer. The short conversation Luke and I had really stuck with me. *What did I think about God?* I went to an Episcopal church after I was adopted, but never really listened. As soon as I could *not* go to church, I stayed home. I went to my bedside table and pushed aside all the junk that had accumulated there.

There it was, shoved way in the back with a green fake leather cover. I brought it into my bed and sat in the glow of my side table light.

The New Testament. What makes it "New?" I didn't even know the most basic things. I made a mental note to ask Luke. The first night I just flipped through it.

As he said, there were four books on Jesus' life. I found the one with the title Luke. It turns out that Luke was the author of that section. Over the next few nights, I read about Jesus. Every night was filled with emotion. Reading about his birth, life, and death, I developed a deep connection I never expected. I fell in love with Jesus. By the end, I was filled with fury when the people chose Barnabas to be let go over Him. Tears ran down my face when He breathed his last breath, and joy beamed from my eyes when Jesus rose from the dead and went to his friends.

On Friday, I was waiting at our booth. I wasn't sure I wanted to talk about the changes in me this week. When Luke came in, I flashed hot. He sat down. We ordered the special and sat staring at each other for a second or two.

"So, I read Luke in the New Testament this week," I blurted. I shifted uncomfortably in my seat and put my hands under my thighs.

"I was hoping you would." He smiled. "What did you think?"

"Okay, call me crazy if you want. I think I believe it. Can a person change like that in a week?" I asked and waited for the teasing.

"That's amazing," he said, coming over to my side of the booth. He hugged me. "I felt the same when I first started reading about Jesus' life."

He blushed a little. My eyes went to my lap, and he backed up a little. "This is very cool, Beth. Did you read any other parts?"

"No, it took me all week just to get through Luke. I do want to read more." I looked at him. "Can I ask you some questions about the Bible?"

The waitress brought our food, and he hopped back over to the other side of the table. "Thanks, Janette," Luke said. As she turned and walked away, he turned to me. "Of course, I would love to help, if I can."

"Why is it the *New* Testament?"

"Well, I think the bible you have just has the Psalms and the New Testament." He looked at me with questioning eyes. I nodded, and he went on.

"That is only part of the Bible. There is a New Testament and an Old Testament. The Old Testament is a lot of what happened before Jesus, and the New Testament is the life of Jesus and what happened after his death for several years. What you read before, Revelation, is a prophecy about how this world will end."

Satisfied, I plunged my fork into my bowl of green leaves. I asked, "What's with all the different sections about Jesus' life? Why not just one?"

"My thoughts are because different people give different perspectives. Mark, John, Matthew, and Luke all had different jobs before they chose to follow Jesus, and all had a different outlook on life and what was important."

"I can understand that," I said. My thoughts trailed off while I chewed my salad. "Any thoughts on what section I should read this week?" I asked, my eyes focused on what I was eating.

"Maybe you could read Acts. That tells about what happened to Jesus's disciples in the time after He went back into Heaven.

"That sounds good. I'll do that." With that, we ate quietly for a while. I asked him how work went this week, and the conversation took on a lighter note as he told me about a client with a big, beautiful house.

Week after week, that is how our lunches went. A little bible talk, then day-to-day stuff.

Then one Friday in mid-October, "Can I meet your girls?" Luke asked, standing in front of me after we finished our lunch.

I froze as I slipped my arms into my coat sleeves. Luke took one step with his long legs and was right in front of me. He wrapped his arm around my waist and pulled me close.

His face inches from mine. I wouldn't have remembered my name if you had asked me. He pressed his lips to mine. It sent tingles all the way to the tips of my ears when he kissed me. His hand on my cheek sent a wave of instability through my limbs. I leaned into him.

Our second first kiss, right there in the middle of the restaurant, was a public declaration of his feelings for me. When the kiss ended, he looked at me as if no one else was there. He said, "I would like to get to know all of you."

Dazed, it took a moment to find my voice. I wanted to scream *Yes and meet me in the backseat of your car!* But what came out was, "I'll have to let you know." I put my hand on his chest.

He nodded, "I understand."

I had more than myself to think about. I turned and walked out to my car. On the ride home, I turned off my sex starved brain and tried to look at this budding relationship, and if I wanted to present it to the children. By the time I got to the girls' school, I knew the answer was yes.

After the girls bounded up the stairs and were snacking in front of the television, I called Luke.

"Hello?" he answered.

"Hi Luke, here's what I was thinking. We skip next Friday and instead you come over for lunch Saturday here at my apartment." I took a deep breath. "The girls and I plan to make pancakes and bacon."

"Isn't that breakfast?" I could hear his smile in the question.

"We're wild and crazy like that. I figured you should know right away." He laughed and agreed. "Really, though, you should be warned. I don't censor the girls when we talk. They could say anything. Please feel free to not answer any questions they have."

"Perfect, I can't wait."

"See you then." I hung up the phone, covered my face with my hands, and sank to the floor just as I did that first time he kissed me on the cheek so long ago.

On Wednesday evening, as the girls and I sat around our spaghetti and meatballs, I took a deep breath and said, "Girls, I want to have a pancake party this weekend." Jess whooped with joy; she loved pancake parties. "An old friend of mine is going to come and join us."

With that, they stopped and looked at me with wondering eyes. "Who?" Jen asked when it was clear I would not give any other info.

"His name is Luke. I've been back in touch with him for a few weeks and think you guys should meet him." I wished I could have said it with my eyes closed. I've dated people over the years, but I have never brought anyone to our home.

"He was Uncle Tom's best friend growing up. He used to live right down the road from Grammy." I could feel my face blush a bit. "He went into the military and then his mom moved away. Luke and his mom came into Dr. Massie's office for a checkup, and we reconnected." I was over-explaining. I was more nervous than I expected. I decided to shut up and see if they had any actual questions.

"Okay," Julie said.

"I don't care. I love pancakes." Jess shrugged.

Jen was giving me the side-eye. "How do you feel about that?" I asked, looking at her.

"Should be interesting," she said with the smart-ass grin she inherited from me.

Chapter Thirty-Three

Saturday at exactly twelve-thirty, the doorbell rang. The girls scrambled around as they raced to see who would get there first to open the door. I came around the corner just in time to see them open it. All three girls looked far up to face this tall man standing in front of them.

He had his classic melting smile on when I introduced the girls. "Nice to meet all of you." He handed us each a different colored flower. We blushed and thanked him.

"Come in," I said, and led the way to the kitchen.

"Would you like an apron?" Jen asked Luke, holding one out that had pink flowers and white ruffles. She stared him down, daring him to say no.

"Of course," without missing a beat, he put it over his head and tied it around the back. "I wouldn't want to get my shirt stained." Jess covered a smile with her hand.

Julie cooked the bacon on one side of the stove. Jen and I set the table and sugared berries. Jess poured the batter into the pan, and when it came time to flip the pancake, Luke would take the pan and toss the pancake into the air. Most of the time, it worked out, and there were shouts of joy and clapping.

One time, the pancake missed the pan and splat like a cartoon on the floor. There was a half second of silence as all eyes went to me. I started laughing, and so did everyone else.

Once everything was cooked, and the table set, we ate with an ease I did not expect.

"Mom says you knew Uncle Tommy in school?" Jess asked.

That was all Luke needed to launch into a flurry of stories about their uncle. Jen said she can't wait until Christmas when Uncle Tommy would visit from North Carolina so she could tease him with this new information.

After lunch, we moved into the living room. At the moment, Luke was sitting on the floor with Jen. She was showing him her magazine collection. Mostly they were subjects you wouldn't think a fourteen-year-old would be interested in. Time, People, Newsweek, but then also Rolling Stone, and Tiger Beat. "I thought this one was particularly interesting." She grabbed a Newsweek from February of this year. "We are children of divorce, did you know?"

"Yes, I did. Your mom told me the first time we met for lunch to catch up."

"Are you divorced?"

"No," Luke answered.

"You've never been married? That seems weird. You seem nice enough," Jen said.

Kill me now. I closed my eyes. *I should have told them more about Luke.*

"I was married. My wife died three years ago," he said without sadness or irritation at being asked so many personal questions. I was glad I at least warned Luke.

Jen was looking at me now. "Mom, you could have told us that."

"You could have stopped asking questions when he said he wasn't divorced."

"You're right," Jen said to me, then turned to Luke. "Sorry."

"No problem," he said.

Jen went back to chatting about her magazines. I caught Luke's eye across the coffee table. I tightened my neck and pulled my bottom lip down in an *eek* expression. He tilted his head and smiled back.

After a few more conversations, he stood and announced he had to leave. All three girls whined, and Jess grabbed his leg. "Can you come back tomorrow?" she asked.

Luke looked at me, and I shrugged. "We were headed to Smithfield's Orchard tomorrow to pick apples. You're welcome to come along," I said. Then I added, "If you aren't busy," in case he needed an out.

"I love apple picking. Should I meet you guys there or pick you up?"

"Pick us up." Jen decided for everyone. "We want to go in your car." Everyone looked at me again to see what I would say.

"Sounds great. How about ten?"

"I'll be here," he said. His hands were in his pockets, and he was looking right into my eyes.

The words felt like more than he would be here to pick us up. Almost like he was telling me he wanted to be here, for me, forever. Goosebumps prickled my skin.

We all stood at the door until he drove off. Later, on the couch, Julie was laying with her head in my lap finishing up *Are You There God, It's Me Margret* by Judy Blume. Jess and Jen were chatting about their outfits for tomorrow while putting the magazines back in order. I attempted to listen to them, but I was in Lala Land over the way the day had gone. I sat there for a long time, stroking Julie's hair as we both processed the day in our own way.

Sunday at ten sharp, the doorbell rang. When we opened the door, he was standing there with brown paper bags that had their names on them. Each bag sported a different hand-drawn design, something specific he learned about them yesterday.

Reader Julie's bag had a girl's face buried in a book, so you only saw eyes and hair. Wild Jen's had a zooming pair of roller skates. Dancer Jess's bag had a ballerina in a tutu. Squeals rang out. Inside the bags, the girls found a Hershey's bar and a pet rock.

The day was crisp, and so were the apples. As I helped Jess grab some apples with a long stick that had a basket on the end, I heard Jen say to Luke, "I like to date girls."

To his credit, Luke turned towards her and put his hands to his chest, "Oh my goodness, me too!" He said it with the enthusiasm of one of her friends she just told she liked chocolate ice cream.

Her right hook caught his upper arm, and he faked being hurt. "I just thought you should know. Some people don't like that about me."

"They can suck an egg," Luke said.

Jen looked back at me with a ruffled brow and pointed at him with her thumb. She had a smile that said *can you believe this guy*. I smiled and nodded. She turned back and made a running jump for his high back. He grabbed her up with ease and comfort, as if he had known her all her life. Jess ran up and grabbed his hand.

Next to me, Julie tilted her head and whispered, "Ma, I think he's a keeper." My heart swelled with feelings I didn't know if I was ready for.

We filled the bags and when we got to the scale, Luke paid for it all. I tried to stop him, but he insisted.

On the way home, the girls were quietly eating their apple-cinnamon doughnuts in the back seat. I dared to reach across the front seat and touch Luke's hand. He looked at me with what felt like love. *Was I just imagining all this? The ease, the warmth, the feeling that this was special.*

Filled with the need to keep him near, I asked, "Luke, if you came up for burgers and chips, we could make an apple pie for dessert." The girls stopped munching and burned a hole in the back of Luke's head, waiting for his answer.

I went on, "You and Jess could cook the burgers while I cut the apples, and Julie and Jen could spice them. I already made a pie crust this morning."

"That sounds like the best lunch ever," he said with a quick look in the back seat. "I wouldn't miss it for the world."

Luke stayed a little later than Saturday. When he left, we made a date for Friday morning and the girls begged him to come back on Saturday. He said he would be there.

So it went on for weeks. We would see each other most Fridays for lunch and then spend time with the girls on Saturdays. We all even started going to Luke's church together on Sundays. I knew I was in deep on Thanksgiving.

The girls and I sat around my kitchen table with my parents. Julie said, "Something's missing."

My first thought was *Luke.*

"Luke," Jess said, and the girls agreed.

"When will we get to see Luke again?" My dad asked. I was shocked. He never wants to meet anyone. "You should invite him to Christmas Eve."

"Okay," I said as slowly as my racing heart would allow. My dad wanted to see Luke, my kids missed him, and I loved him. *Whose life was this?*

Chapter Thirty-Four

"Luke," I laid it out one day in December over our ham and mashed potato specials. "I have fallen in love with you. I love you alone, I love you with my kids, I think about you constantly."

"Beth, I love you too. You make me so happy, and I love your girls." He ran his fingers through his hair like he did when he was nervous. "I hope this isn't weird to say. I honestly never thought I would feel this way again. I was prepared to be alone for the rest of my life. God had other plans, and I knew them as soon as I walked into that dentist's office." His soft eyes curved with his smile made me go steamy.

"Honestly, I've never felt this way. I never loved Matt, not even in the beginning. I was just going along with what was expected after a misstep. I know why I went through that now. It was for the three stars of my heart." I touched my hand to my chest.

I went on. "I wasn't even sure I could love until Millie and John. I never even thought love really existed." I looked down at my potato pile. By this time, he knew just about everything about my life before we were teens together. "When we were teens, I was still pretty messed up from being tossed around. I'm so happy God brought us to each other again."

We half stood and met for a kiss over the table.

"My dad wants you to come to Christmas Eve dinner," I said, changing the subject as we sat back in our seats.

"Really? Sounds great. My mom has invited you guys to our day after Christmas party, too."

"Sounds great," I repeated in the same tone. "I can't wait to meet your stepfamily." The rest of the lunch was spent talking about them.

At my parents' house Christmas Eve, Tom was there with his wife and kids; nine-year-old Tommy and eight-year-old Justin.

"Oh my goodness, Uncle Tommy, I can't believe you took alcohol from Luke's house and drank it behind our apartment!" Jess blurted as she ran up to him, only one arm out of the sleeve of her coat. His kids gasped and covered their mouths.

"Don't repeat my mistakes," he said in the way grown-ups talk to children when they hope they don't repeat a behavior they themselves loved when they were young.

Then he pointed his long-neck Molson in my direction. "I was not the only one sneaking alcohol from my friend's house."

As I took off my coat, I mouthed "thank you" with closed eyes. I nodded to the girls in confirmation.

"How did we never hear about this?" Jen asked.

"You never asked." A smile beaming from my face.

"What else haven't you told us?" Jen asked.

"Plenty!" I raised my eyebrows and took a sip of the spiked eggnog my mother handed me.

After more questions of antics and stories of what we have done over the years, we all sat down to eat the amazing dinner my mother insists on preparing by herself every year. She says it is the only time she gets to go all out, and she loves every minute of it.

Christmas day was quiet. The girls and I opened presents and then watched television. Our Christmas meal was always leftovers from Grammy's the night before.

I noticed Julie fidgeting with her fingernails on the way to Luke's family's house on the day after Christmas. When she sighed for the third time, I asked, "Is everything okay?"

"I forgot to ask Luke what we should call his mother and stepfather?" Julie always felt more comfortable knowing as much about a new situation as possible. If she knew how long it took to get there, how long we were staying, and who was going to be there, she would have a much better time.

On Christmas Eve, Luke explained the party norms to her with compassion. He was sure to remind her that things were slightly different each year and if she was uncomfortable in any way, we would help.

Taking a hand off the steering wheel, I touched her arm to help steady her hands. "I think we should call them Mr. and Mrs. Desmond. Does that sound good?"

Her eyebrows and forehead relaxed. "Yes, sorry, I should have known that," she said, looking at her lap.

"It is fine to ask questions, especially to me. You know I love them." Julie brightened at this. She knew it was true.

Luke's mom and Paul's family were there, along with various other family members. The girls had a great time with the other kids, and I had a wonderful time meeting Luke's new family.

Elsa and Paul never had children of their own, but he had four children with his first wife before she passed away. Most of them were scattered across the United States, but his youngest son, Darren, was there for the party. He was twenty years old, and in college for civil engineering.

Getting a second glass of wine, I had to smile, noticing Luke and Julie on the couch chatting together. The easy way he has slipped into our lives feels right. I walked over to them.

"How are things over here?" I asked.

"Great," Julie said with a wide smile, then bounced off before I could say another word.

I snuggled in next to Luke. "Great party."

"Ya, I really love when everyone is together," he said, wrapping his arms around me and kissing the top of my head.

Chapter Thirty-Five

"Happy early New Year," I said to the girls when Luke and I left for our party.

"Happy early New Year," the girls and my mom chirped back.

At the party put on by Luke's company, there were seas of fruit and veggie platters, meats and cheeses, and shrimp cocktails. Slices of cake were laid out at ten-thirty. Wine and beer flowed like water. Just before midnight, Champagne was passed around. When the clock struck twelve, we toasted out 1980 and rang in 1981. Luke kissed me. We whispered Happy New Year softly to each other, just like everyone else in the ocean of people.

With his forehead on mine and my eyes closed, I heard "I love you, Beth."

My eyes flew open. "I love you too," I said, blinking away tears. Every time he said it sent shockwaves through me. Just a few months ago, he wasn't even a thought. Now it felt like he had been there the whole time.

"I have loved you again almost from the first moment in the dentist's office," he said with a smile. "I love you, your kids, and your whole family." He still had me close to him.

"Same here," I said. "We all love you. The girls talk about you non-stop."

"I don't want to be away from you or the girls anymore. I had a chat with Julie a few days ago. I told her I wanted to be part of your family."

I stood there in his arms with my mouth open. I may have stopped breathing. Luke continued. "She said she and the girls would love that." He broke his embrace as he spoke and took a box from his pocket. "I told her I was going to ask you to marry me tonight." He went down on one knee.

My hands flew to my face. "Oh my goodness," I whispered.

He opened the box. "Beth, will you marry me?"

Tears and mascara streamed down my face. Somehow, I got out, "Yes."

With both of us in tears, he slid the ring onto my shaking finger. He came in close, lifted me off the ground, and spun me with a long, deep kiss.

Applause and shouts rose all around us. I looked around and realized that everyone was looking at us. Luke set me down and raised our joined hands in triumph, and then we took a great bow. As people clapped, we ran off to the parking lot.

As we walked to the car, we were already kissing. He put his arm over my shoulder and pressed his hand to the top of the car. The other arm went around my waist and he pulled me into him as he bent down to kiss me, deep and full. My hands went up his back to try to bring myself closer to him, even though there was no space between us. Our lips parted and Luke said, "We need to go get the kids."

My eyes flew open. "What?" I asked, tilting my head, "Why?" I planned to race home and rip off his clothes. We hadn't yet had sex and even before the proposal, I thought this night would be perfect.

Looking into my eyes, he said, "Because if we don't leave right now, I am going to make love to you right here." His voice was deep, and his arm got tighter around my waist. Hot sparks shot up my spine. "I want our first time together to be as man and wife." He meant what he said.

Mustering all my strength, I gently pushed him away and straightened my dress. "Okay. You're serious about this?"

"I think it may have been the hardest thing I've ever had to say." He took a step back and ran both hands through his hair, sighed, and then laughed at himself.

I laughed and turned to open the car door. "Do you think they'll be up?" I asked as I pulled it open.

"Julie has probably told them all about tonight. Ya, I think they'll be up." He took the door from me and helped me in.

"This ring is gorgeous," I said as we drove. I held it out in front of me to see it better in the dark car. Sapphires and diamonds glistened off the passing streetlights.

"It was my grandmother's, and her mother-in-law's ring before that." His chest swelled as he spoke.

"Luke, oh my goodness, I love that." This was no trinket. I didn't ask the question that blinked through my mind for a second. *Had Daily worn this too?* I put the thought out of my head. Even if she had, she had been amazing to Luke, and I was grateful for that.

"My mom gave that to me two weeks ago when I told her I was going to ask you to marry me." Taking my hand, he interlaced our fingers. My heart pinged selfishly a little, knowing for sure now that the ring was only mine.

We drove up and saw a light in the window with two angels looking into the dark night. When they saw the car drive up, they scooted away from the glass. Before we were even out of the car, they were on the porch.

Julie and Jen were jumping up and down like six-year-olds. "Did he ask you? Are we a family now?" They called.

"Yes!" I called back as I climbed out of the car in my high heels, trying to avoid the snowbanks.

"That would have been awkward if I chickened out," Luke called over the hood from the driver's side.

They cheered and hugged each other and ran back inside to tell my parents. We followed them up the stairs and Luke whispered from behind me, "I also had a chat with your dad to make my intentions known. That was about a week before Christmas."

I turned to him and kissed his forehead. "Boy, you are just full of surprises."

I walked into the living room with the silliest schoolgirl grin. My dad was sitting in his chair, of course. My mom jumped off the couch, dropping the knitting back into its basket, and hugged my neck. "We are so happy for you two." Then she went to hug Luke.

My dad got up and shook Luke's hand, then kissed me on the cheek. "Good Luck kids." He cracked half a smile and went back to the chair.

"What did he say?" Jen asked.

"Did he get down on one knee right there, in front of everyone?" Julie asked.

As we were answering them, Jess came out of the bedroom. "Hey guys, why didn't you wake me?"

"We tried." Jen rolled her eyes. "Grandpa's air horn couldn't wake you up."

Jess laughed. She knew it was true. She came and stood in front of Luke. She leaned over, practically nose to nose, and grabbed his cheeks in her hand.

"Did you ask?" she asked. He nodded, and she turned to me, "Did you say yes?" I nodded. She stood straight with her hands up to the ceiling. "YES!" she called to the heavens and wiggled her twelve-year-old body onto my lap.

Just a few minutes later, the girls were yawning, and we all stood to say goodnight. Luke dropped us all home with a promise to return for lunch tomorrow.

One after another, dates were set, and plans were made. We all wanted to be a family as soon as possible, and with no reason to wait, we set a date of January twenty-fourth. Just enough time to tell the people we wanted to share the day with and get dresses for the kids and myself.

A few days before the wedding, Luke and I were out for dinner. "Do you think we should have more kids?" he asked as we waited for our dessert.

"I've been thinking about it." I thought of it often since he told me he loved me back in

November. Little sweet Lukes toddling around would be the cutest thing. But what would the girls think about being so much older? Was I too old to chase after rampant youngsters? Did I want to leave my job? Life was good and settled, but still, it would be worth it.

"I want you to know I am on board with whatever you want. Kids, no kids. Our lives together with the girls will be perfect."

Our pie came with two forks. As he dug into the flaky crust and the rich cherry filling, he looked at me for my thoughts.

"I have gone over it and over it," I said, digging into the opposite side of the pie. "I think maybe we should just see what happens for a while. Not try to stop anything from happening," trying to get my point across without actually saying the words sex or birth control. "And if it happens, it happens. If not, then that will be okay, too."

He nodded his head, pointing his fork at me. "That sounds really great. I like that plan."

When Pastor Evers agreed to marry us, I was so honored. She had been a mentor of mine for a while now, and the girls really looked up to her.

I found a straight, plum-colored, floor-length dress with long organza sleeves and a high neckline.

I loved the way it made my feathered brunette hair and blue eyes shine with my raspberry-colored lips.

The girls wore dresses that had poofy skirts and came to their knees. Julie in pale blue, Jen in cotton candy pink, and Jess in white. Luke wore a black suit and tie he bought new for the occasion.

On the twenty-fourth, we had a small ceremony with just some family, people from church, and friends from work. Patty, Betty, Mark, and Donna were there. Tom in North Carolina and Debbie in California couldn't make it with such short notice. I had tried to contact Judy over the years with various phone numbers my mother gave me, but she never returned my calls. This occasion was no different.

We had our reception in the church basement. The night went by in a blur of photos, friends, food, and drink. Our friend brought his record collection, and everyone danced through the night with albums ranging from Micheal Jackson to Led Zepplin to The Talking Heads.

Somewhere between the Hustle and The Funky Chicken, I sat down to drink some water. I caught sight of Mom and Dad dancing to *Easy* by The Commodores.

Dad's such a big stoic man, but he loves deeply. The way he held her and guided her around the dance floor, I could see how in love they still were. I was overcome with gratitude towards them. They took me from a horrible place all those years ago and gave me such love that I almost forgot about the time before. Sometimes in my teens, I would think *it is too late. I can't learn to love. I can't truly love anyone.* Teens can be so dramatic. I had no reference point before them. I learned to love them and accept their love.

Married to Matt, I wondered if I would spend my life in a loveless marriage. But no, when I finally pulled up my big-girl pants and left Matt, it was at my parents' house that again I was shown how it was supposed to be.

I never thought I'd have a day like that day, with a man that loved and respected not only me, but my daughters. Why God protected my heart so carefully and brought me to this point, I will only know in the afterlife. But God plucked me out of an awful place and put me with these two parents who could play a prominent role in my life.

As the song finished, I crossed the dance floor and hugged them both. "Thank you," I said.

They looked at each other. "For what?" my mom asked.

"For adopting me. God knows I gave you a lot of grief. Thank you so much for loving me." We had a deep long hug, and we were all wet-eyed and sniffy when we let go.

My dad put his hand on my head. "You were a tough nut to crack," he said with a smile. "We love you too."

Around eleven o'clock, Luke and I danced the last dance to the song "*Reunited,*" and there wasn't a dry eye in the house.

We said goodbye to the girls out on the icy sidewalk as they piled into my parents' car. "Bye. Have a good night. I love you," we said to all in the car.

Wrapped in two coats and having exchanged my heels for boots, I was still chilly as I waved after them. When we could no longer see them, we got into Luke's car and drove to my apartment.

"I have to admit I'm a little nervous," I called out from my tiny bathroom as I slipped into something a little more comfortable. Standing there in my tiny bathroom, I realized it was *our* tiny bathroom now.

Everything was fun until now. Now things were real. *We're married. He lives here. We are about to have sex.* I grabbed the sink and took a couple of deep breaths.

I took a step back to look at my lingerie. *Focus on the reality of how amazing he is. Sexy, strong, independent, sexy, encouraging, loving, sexy, good kisser, skillful hands, sexy. Okay, I'm back.* I walked out of the bathroom and turned the corner to stand on the threshold of the bedroom.

“Hello, Mrs. Marcome,” he said as I came into the room. He was lying on the bed, totally naked, with just a sheet covering him. The sheet wasn’t hiding anything. I could see his excitement through the thin white fabric. I wore a little red silky number and still felt a little shy. I wasn’t sure how to take the next step.

Luke sat up and patted the bed beside him. When I sat next to him, he brought me down on the bed. Wrapped in a bear hug, he kissed me deeply. My fingers twirled in his chest hairs. His hands explored their way all over my glossy lingerie, and passion flowed from us both. Sighs and moans escaped our lips with desperate kisses, silencing them only for a moment.

Luke brought his lips to my ears and whispered, “I love you, Elizabeth Marcome.” Then he ran his lips and tongue down my neck. He looked at me. “I never want you to be anything you don’t want to be,” he said, and continued his kisses.

Bringing my lips to his ears, I told him, “You have always been true and honest.” I stopped to nibble his lobe. “I always want to be yours.” He grabbed my face and kissed me with heat. My name escaped his lips in a whisper.

Later that night, I lay there nuzzled under his chin, riding his heaving inhales and exhales. “That was unlike anything ever," I told him as I got my breath back.

"Mmmm, I have no words. I think you broke my brain," he said. Laughing, he flipped me onto my back. "The only thing in control now is you know who." His eyes looked down, and I saw what he meant. He was at attention, ready to play again; two more sessions that night and we fell asleep just before four—spent.

We woke at about ten the next morning and started all over again. Eventually, we dragged ourselves, still inseparable, to the shower, then gathered our things to pick up the girls.

Chapter Thirty-Six

We decided to ski in the White Mountains of New Hampshire for a family honeymoon. It was the first time the girls and I had been skiing. No one could contain giggles, not even me, on the bunny slope as Luke tried to teach me to turn. Every single time I landed on my butt. Julie was a pro from the start.

Regardless of skill, or lack thereof, every day we were on the slopes. Every night we ate dinner in the great hall and were cozied down in the evenings with books on the overstuffed chairs.

There was a big square-dance on our last night. We doe-see-doe'd and swung our partners late into the night.

Everyone woke at nine on Saturday morning and packed the car for the journey home. We stopped for lunch at a greasy spoon before hopping on the highway. With happy hearts and full tummies, we started home.

As we drove home, the girls fell asleep. I reached over and took Luke's hand. In a low voice spoken through my smile, "You are coming to live in my home, our home. It's unreal." Tears filled my eyes. My hands flew to my face to cover them. "I thought I was happy before you walked into the office. I thought our lives were complete. I didn't know." Luke pulled the car over. He slid across the bench seat and put his arms around me.

Jess woke up. "Is everything alright?" she asked.

"Perfect," I said, wiping my eyes. Satisfied, she dozed off again.

The next few weeks were interesting. Getting used to living together differs greatly from visiting. Luke was very understanding of a teenage girl's need for the bathroom and the telephone.

"A major buying feature of our next place will be two bathrooms," he called from the hallway to anyone who could hear as he waited his turn.

Soon we settled into an easy pattern. The girls kept going to my mom's after school during the week and Luke commuted to his job. Luke's house sold two months after the wedding, and we were house hunting.

Our real estate agent showed us everything from high-end houses to handyman specials for months. Finally, we found a ranch house with four small bedrooms and, thankfully, two bathrooms on three-quarters of an acre.

It wasn't powder blue with a white picket fence, but it was just right for us. It was in a nice neighborhood with other children and the girls could still go to the same school. We moved in on July 1, 1981.

30 Years Ago

Chapter Thirty-Seven

The week of Halloween, I had a pile of candy on top of my usual groceries for the neighborhood kids that would come to my door on Thursday. Standing in line to pay, my eye caught a magazine cover. Like everyone in the check-out line, I read the covers as I waited my turn.

Luke and I often joke about the article titles on the covers. Today, alone in line, one title made me stop and read it. "What to say to your man to have him begging for more."

To my surprise, the article was about bedroom talk. I was blushing in the supermarket reading it, but couldn't wait to find the right time to use it. I waited until we were on our mini vacation after Thanksgiving.

On Thanksgiving, we ate with Luke's parents. On Friday morning, the kids stayed there, and we headed off to the White Mountains of New Hampshire.

Feeling aroused at the words in my head and blushing at the thought of saying them, I decided not to wait. I slid across to the middle of the seat. He smiled as I came close but didn't take his eyes off the road.

"Hi," I said deep and quiet in his ear and gave it a nibble then kissed his neck.

He tilted his head to rest on my forehead. "What is going on here? We still have an hour's drive."

I thought back to the article I read. I felt a little funny, but I went for it. "I can't help myself. The thought of what you'll do to me when we are alone is too much," I said. I slid my hand up his leg and let loose my carefully crafted words.

"Whoa, whoa," he swerved the car for a second. "Language, young lady. I'm driving," he said in his playful way.

Snickering, "What? There are no kids to hear us. I thought it would be a little fun to let out some dirty words." I kissed his neck up and into his hairline. "Tell me what you feel," I said.

With a full smile and eyes glued to the road, he said, "I feel like I'm not going to make it to the cottage without having to stop."

"That isn't what I meant."

"I feel like if I don't pull over, I'll get into an accident."

A small laugh escaped me between neck kisses. One of his hands came off the steering wheel and rose up my skirt. "Oh, is this why you had a skirt on today? You little Vixen, how long have you been planning this?"

"Since you said we should get away over the long weekend. It has been all I can think about."

Luke left the highway, turning off the next exit onto a busy road. His eyes searched for something. A left turn at the light onto a lesser traveled street, and he found it. We pulled in and he shut off the engine. We made love there: Passion flowing in daylight behind an abandoned gas station.

A release like no other happened between us, with naughty words, shudders, and curled toes. Then we were quiet, heaving and sweating in our clothes.

"Where did that come from?" he asked after he regained the speech part of his brain.

"Cosmo," I told him, and we both laughed.

"Fun," he said, catching his breath.

"I felt a little weird getting started, but, yes, it was fun."

We straightened our clothes and got back on the road and arrived at our cottage an hour later.

Still worked up from the quicky in the car, we dropped our bags to the floor and gave the beds a test run. Then we went in search of something to eat. After dinner, we brought food back to the room and planned not to go out again until Sunday.

In early December 1983, I had a familiar feeling. First, I would be starving, and then nauseous. After two missed days of my period, I went to the drugstore and got a pregnancy test. They resembled a kid's chemistry set, and I didn't trust my results. I made an appointment with my doctor. He called later to confirm the positive test results I got at home. I did a private little happy dance there on the kitchen floor.

Pregnant. Pregnant with Luke's baby. None of my life had gone the way I ever imagined it. I looked around and thought how unpredictably God had brought me through this life. I was alone when the doctor called, and I decided to keep my precious secret until Christmas.

We were going to do the same thing we did each year: my parents on Christmas Eve and his mom's the day after Christmas. Christmas day was reserved for us, together as a family.

I tripped over my words in those two weeks, almost spilling the beans. My smile told everyone I had a secret. As it was Christmas time, I could say, "It's the joy of the season."

Christmas Day came. All the gifts were opened, and we gathered in the kitchen to make Christmas breakfast. As we sat around the table, we talked and shoveled maple-covered waffles into our mouths. This was the perfect time.

"Everyone, I want to say something." With all eyes on me, I began a speech I had been working on for two weeks. "The past three Christmases together have been so wonderful. I have loved every minute of being a family, the five of us." My smile grew so wide when I looked at Luke. I could tell he knew what I was going to say next by the color of his cheeks.

With tears in my eyes, I continued, "But this is the last Christmas that it will be just us." I held my breath and squeezed my eyes shut. "I'm pregnant." I let the words sit there on the table with the fluffy yellow breakfast squares and sticky syrup.

The room erupted.

Luke hooted and jumped up. He lifted me with a hug and spun me around the kitchen. Then set me down gently. "Oh no, did I hurt you?"

"No," I said with a smile. "The baby and I are fine." He hugged me again.

The girls went crazy. They came over to hug me, too. There was a jumble of questions like, "How long have you known?" and "Why didn't you tell us sooner?"

Jess put her hands on my belly and said, "Hello in there." We all laughed.

I couldn't help thinking about how different this time was compared to the three times I told Matt I was pregnant. There was no hooting or hugging then. There was no happiness or excitement, only disappointment. I put it out of my head and focused on the love and happy anticipation of this moment.

Chapter Thirty-Eight

I worked until I was eight months pregnant. The office gave me a small baby shower on my last day. Cute yellow onesies, rattles, stuffed toys, and mountains of diapers left with me, along with big hugs and many tears.

The girls were up and down about the pregnancy. Julie and Jen, eighteen and seventeen years old, both were too busy to think much of it. Julie was graduating and on her way to a teaching college in New Hampshire. Jen was busy with various volunteer projects, friends, and school. Now and then they would comment on how big my tummy was getting.

Now the baby was moving all the time. Jess always referred to the baby as her little bundle. She would talk to my tummy and tell it about the house or what color the sunset was. She would sing lullabies and show tunes. She would also tell her version of how the girls met Luke, which included the great pancake drop of 1980.

Having a baby in the eighties differed vastly from in the sixties. The girls and my mom were there in the early stages of labor. Luke was with me the whole time, right there in the delivery room. When the contractions kicked in, I was screaming and crushing his giant hand in mine. After I pushed for two hours, the doctor told me it was no use.

"The baby isn't going anywhere, and you are both in danger. You need a cesarean," he said.

They told Luke he needed to wait in the waiting room, but he made a fuss and the doctor allowed him to be in the operating room. As Luke and I prepped, the drugs they gave me numbed me nicely and dazed me a bit. The doctor and nurse tugged me around behind the curtain.

Luke was at my face chatting about dinner. "Do you think they have a big, juicy steak in the cafeteria?" he asked.

It may have been the dope, but my head filled with laughter. "I think the best you will get is a dry hamburger."

"That won't do." He smiled at me.

"He is out," the doctor said.

"He?" Luke asked. Tears filled both our eyes.

"You have a son," I whispered through my daze and wondered where the cry was.

"I have a son," he whispered back.

My attention turned to the flutter of activity at the baby's table. After what seemed like many agonizing quiet minutes, which were only seconds, I heard the glorious sound of my newborn baby boy's cry. There is nothing better for a mother's ears. I let out the breath I had been holding.

The nurse gave our son to Luke, and I got to touch his face. "Hello little one," I said to him. Then to Luke, "He looks so much like you."

Luke beamed a smile I had never seen before. He peppered his son with kisses and spilled them over onto my forehead. I had to go to the recovery room until I could feel my legs. Luke went to my room and sat with the baby.

When I was rolled back to my room, my heart raced at the sight of Luke holding our son. They got me into my bed and left us alone. Luke handed me the little floppy bundle. "What should we name him?" he asked.

I looked at our son's scrunchy face. "What do you think of Jordan? I think he looks like a Jordan."

"I was thinking the same thing." I gave him a side eye to see if he was just teasing me. "No really," he laughed. "He and I have been up here for a while and had some time to talk to each other. Looking into his little face, I thought he was a Jordan."

The girls were surprised to learn they had a brother. "I thought you could only make girls," Jen said.

Jordan slept in our room because we were short on space. We bought him a crib and yellow bedding. Before long, he was sleeping through the night.

When Julie left for college, we did the bedroom shuffle. Jen kept the bigger bedroom. Jess went to Julie's old room, and Jordan got Jess's.

27 Years Ago

Chapter Thirty-Nine

One afternoon when Jordan was two, we were at the supermarket. He would stand in the cart and play the toss-out game. After stooping down to get the tossed loaf of bread, for the second time, I became dizzy. I checked out right away and drove home.

Jess was at school, and Luke was at work. I put Jordan in the playpen and got the groceries put away. I came into the living room and put on the television to watch my soaps while I lay down on the couch.

I must have fallen asleep because I woke up and realized it was four o'clock. Jordan was asleep too. I turned my attention to the burning sensation raging in my chest and stomach. I ran to the bathroom and was thrilled to see the toilet I cleaned this morning. Clinging to it, I revisited my lunch.

As I walked back through the kitchen to get a drink of water, I checked the calendar. This probably wasn't pregnancy.

When Luke came home, I was in the bathroom again, enjoying the coolness of the tile.

As soon as he saw me, his smile faded. "You don't look good. Maybe you should go lay down." He kissed my forehead. "I'll feed Jordan and give him a bath."

"Thanks, babe, I think I will. You're the best," I managed to say as I padded off to the bedroom, holding my head. There were a couple more bathroom runs in the night.

In the morning, I asked Luke to take Jordan to my mom and kissed them all goodbye at the door. The next thing I remember was waking in a hospital bed.

I sat up and saw Luke on a chair beside me. He put his hand on my shoulder and popped a pillow behind me. With a fuzzy head and furrowed brow, I asked, "Why am I here?"

He had come home to check on me after dropping off Jordan. I was on the hall floor. When he couldn't wake me, he picked me up and brought me straight to the emergency room. "You had a heart attack," he said. "If I hadn't come home, you would have been dead."

He left my side for a moment and swung the door open. "She's awake in here," he called to the nurses at their station.

"What? A heart attack?" I said as the door opened, "I'm only thirty-nine."

"Good afternoon, Mrs. Marcome. I am Dr. Rewald. Yes, you had a heart attack. A major one, in fact. It damaged sixty percent of your heart. Your husband told us you had Rheumatic Fever as a girl." He went on looking at my folder, not at me. "That illness usually weakens the heart muscle. It is not uncommon to have heart issues at a younger age."

Of all the things I thought could have been wrong with me, a heart attack was not on the list. "I picture heart attacks happening to elderly men clutching their chest and falling to the floor. This was just heartburn or the flu."

"Well, Mrs. Marc-" was all I heard. Darkness came from all around. I couldn't say anything. The ringing in my ears overpowered the doctor's voice, and then nothing.

This time, I woke up with Luke sitting on the bed. "You gotta stop doing that," he said with a soft smile as he stroked my hair. "Your blood pressure tanked, and you passed out."

"It wasn't fun. I'll try not to do that again." I smiled back at him. "Where are the kids?"

Luke told me Jordan stayed with my mom while he was at the hospital. Jess was at school, even though she was worried and distracted.

"Julie and Jen wondered if they should come home, but I said to stay put until we know more. Jordan is a little confused, but he will be okay."

My smile faded. Poor sweet little one. He doesn't understand why I wasn't there.

Two days passed and there was no more passing out or excitement. The medicines they were giving me were helping me feel better. Luke brought Jordan to see me while Jess was in school. He lay there on my stomach and hugged me the whole time.

Luke brought my camera and took some pictures. "No, Luke, I look awful," I whined as he snapped photos. I shielded my face with my hand.

"Impossible," he said, pressing the button, over and over, popping out pictures of Jordan cuddling me. They turned out to be some of the most precious photos I have with him.

After four more days, the doctors let me go home with a strict diet and rest program. I came home on a Monday, and by Saturday I was happily making pancakes for everyone.

After two months, I was cleared to do normal life activities again. I had to eat healthy and exercise regularly to strengthen my heart muscles. Some parts of my heart had died, and I may need surgery down the road, but for now, we focused on diet, exercise, and medicines.

Tonight, for the first time in what felt like years, I could do more than just sleep next to my husband.

We both lay next to each other, staring at the ceiling. "So," he said, drawing out the o, "We have a green light?"

"Yup."

"How do you feel about that?"

"Nervous." I turned my head to see him still looking at the ceiling.

He turned his head to me. "We could wait."

I let out a great laugh as I looked down and saw his full hardness raising the quilt.

"Don't pay any attention to *him*. He has a mind of his own." He covered his other brain with a pillow. "I'm very interested, as you can see. But don't feel pressured. I want you to be ready." Pulling the sheets up to my neck, I turned away from him. He turned to spoon me.

With his arms around me, his breath on my back, and his bare chest against me, I couldn't deny the physical feeling I yearned for. I took his hand and put it under my t-shirt. He used this cue to kiss the back of my neck.

"Proceed with caution," I said.

"I have missed you," he said in my ear when he entered me. We moved together, ready to stop if I thought it was too much on my heart.

As my heart rate rose near climax, I was scared, but decided an orgasm wouldn't be the worst way to die. Quiet, deep moans filled the room as we both reached the peak of excitement.

After we finished, my hands came to my chest, feeling my racing heart. "Are you okay?" Luke asked, still holding me tight.

"Yes," I said, "Still breathing. That was great. Great, great, great." No other words would come out of my mouth. Then I fell into a hysterical giggle. Luke never let go, and not long after, we fell asleep.

26 Years Ago

Chapter Forty

I jazzercised through the years, with my blue leotard and magenta leggings. I ate a healthy diet, and the years flew by. There were no more heart problems.

Jordan started kindergarten, then first grade, and then second. Julie finished college with a teaching degree. She headed to Seattle for a job teaching at a private school. Jess finished high school and two weeks after she graduated went off to New York to live with Patty and Betty to be a star of the stage.

Jen surprised Luke and me by visiting one day with James, whom she had been dating for three months, and announced they were going to have a baby. She just finished her first year of an RN program in Boston.

"We are going to move in together, but live separately."

When we looked at them, confused, Jen said. "We want to both be there for the baby but not commit to one another. Like roommates."

"Interesting," Luke said. "What if one of you meets someone, falls in love, and wants to move out?"

"We decided we'll take that as it comes. Whoever that might be will have to understand our lifestyle. Our child will always come first," James said.

Committed to parenting together, Jen and James moved in together and Sweet Skye was born on April 27, 1987. She was eight pounds, nine ounces, and had ten fingers, ten toes, and the greenest eyes a baby could have. Not a surprise, Jen and James both had gorgeous green eyes.

24 Years Ago

Chapter Forty-One

Within the blink of an eye, we were all five years older. With Jordan at school all day and Luke at work, I filled my day with cleaning and daytime television. That got old fast.

One night, curled together with Luke watching *Family Ties*, I asked, "Do you think I should go back to work?"

"Do you *want* to go back to work?" Luke asked me.

"I want to do *something*." I pulled at a loose string on the cuff of my shirt. "I just don't know what."

"Don't rush into it," he said. "Give yourself some time to think about what you would love to do." He hugged me closer. "I only want you to do something that you will love doing. We don't need more money, but Jordan and I need you to be happy."

He smiled his eyes down at me and I curled deeper into his chest. I loved him for that, but it didn't make my choice any easier.

Days later, I flip-flopped through thoughts. *Should I go back to school? Should I just stay home? I loved babies. Maybe a daycare? I loved taking photos. Should I open a photo studio? What kind of life did I want for myself and my family?*

One by one, things got scratched off the mental list I created. No to school, not right now, anyway. There wasn't anything I was sure I wanted to learn. No to staying home. I was climbing the walls when Jordan was at school. No to daycare, I didn't want that kind of day-to-day chaos in my home.

Photography stayed on my mind longer. In the end, I decided against that too. Not only because it would be a big investment to upgrade my equipment, but I also didn't enjoy having people strike a pose.

The photos I love most are ones the people didn't see coming. Like the ones with a distracted Jen playing with her dolls at nine years old; or a rare photo of Julie with her head tilted back in a glorious laugh; or Luke and Jess sitting on the couch trying to figure out her math homework from freshman year.

The only places I had ever worked were the diner and the dentist. I called Dr. Massie's office. I picked up the phone, hoping to work a reference letter into the conversation.

The office had always been close-knit. Through the years, the kids' appointments had afforded me opportunities to chat and catch up with the people I knew there. Dr. Massie's son was a dentist there now too. They had changed the name to Massie and Massie Dentistry just two months ago. After chatting a minute with the women in the office, Dr. Massie got onto the phone. He asked me back just after we exchanged greetings. After assuring him that is not why I called, the elder Dr. Massie said, "Elizabeth, please come back to your desk."

My desk. I remembered the family-like atmosphere and decided in that second, "I would love to." I needed two weeks to get things in order here. We thanked each other again and hung up.

When Luke got home, I told him about the call. He hugged me close. "It sounds perfect. That place holds a special place in my heart." He kissed the top of my head.

We told Jordan and gave him the choice between my parent's house or the after-school program at the community center. He would have to ride the bus to school and then to the center. It was a simple choice for my social butterfly: the community center.

It was almost just as easy to slip back into rhythm at the office as it was the first time, only now the computers tripped me up. But it didn't take long before I was booking appointments and printing out receipts like I had been there all along.

Chapter Forty-Two

Just a few weeks on the job, on a Tuesday, my dad came into the office. He never came to the office before, not even for a cleaning. My heart left its God-given place and jumped to my throat. "Dad," I said breathlessly. "What's wrong?" I asked as I rounded the reception desk to be closer to him.

His arms enfolded me and held me in a tight bear hug for a full minute, an act I usually relish because of its scarcity. This time, it terrified me.

He whispered, "Your mom is gone." My limbs went numb, and I released him. His Old Spice filled my head, and the weight of his words pushed me toward the floor. He gripped me tighter and led me to one of the waiting room chairs.

With his giant hands covering mine, he began, "When I woke up this morning, she wasn't in bed. I thought she'd be making breakfast." He took a deep breath in and out through his nose and went on. "I found her on the bathroom floor and called the ambulance. The doctors there said she must have had a stroke. There was nothing they could do." Then he said nothing else.

I bent over with my head in my hands. My hair covered my face when I looked up at him. "Mom died?" was all I could manage to say. He moved my hair behind my ear and nodded, teary-eyed.

Within the week, a plot was acquired, and the funeral home booked. She was laid to rest on a sunny Saturday morning. I know my dad would have jumped in and gone with her if someone had given him the option.

I visited him every day. I didn't need to. He was very good at taking care of himself. I went there to be near my mother's things.

"Sweetheart, could you help me do something?" he asked a week after she'd been gone.

"Of course, Dad. What do you need?"

"I haven't slept in our bed since the day I found her." He crossed his arm over his chest, then swiped his hand down his face. "There is too much of her in here. Can you take her things out?" He blinked away tears.

Emotion pricked my nose and water came to my eyes. "No problem, Dad. Do you want to help? Is there anything specific you want to keep?"

"No, but you should keep anything you want," he said and went to his chair. "We can donate the rest."

I nodded.

It was my first time in their bedroom since she passed. I opened the door and my mother's scent reached out to hug me. I filled my lungs and decided where to start. Frilly magenta curtains covered the windows with a matching comforter on the bed, and two white chairs sat in the corner with lavender throw pillows. I spied the dresser topped with makeup and trinkets.

"I'll start there," I said aloud to no one. Starting with the lipstick, I opened each one and inhaled the oily pigment. The scent brought back the laughing lips of my mom sharing stories around the table over tea.

At first, tossing the lipstick in the garbage felt like betrayal, but as I went on, it felt like freedom. Freeing my mom from her bond to this world. She was no longer in this world to use these things. She was in all of me to be remembered perfectly.

After I cleaned out her dresser, I moved to the closet. I arranged all her clothes on the bed. In the very back of the closet, behind all her blouses and pants suits, I found a few short lace nighties. "Mom, you little minx. When was the last time you wore these?" I smiled to myself and put them in the pile with the rest.

After several trips to the car, I was huffing up the stairs and joked to my dad, "Maybe you should just move. Maybe to a first-floor apartment."

"It has crossed my mind."

After opening both windows in the room and turning the overhead fan on, I stripped the bedding. With a few pushes and pulls, I got the furniture into its new spaces. I made up the bed with clean sheets and an old comforter and switched out the curtains with the ones in my old room. I vacuumed and sprayed a little old spice in the corners of the room and pillows.

"Do you want to come and see before I go, Dad?" He nodded and rose from the chair.

Walking slower than usual, he made his way to the hall. As he walked in and breathed in his cologne, not her scent, his shoulders relaxed a bit. "It's perfect, sweetheart, thank you."

"I hope you can get a good night's rest now. I can bring you some new bedding tomorrow."

He bear-hugged me, "Go be with your guys. You were a big help." I went up on my tippy toes to kiss him on the cheek and left.

I couldn't bring myself to go to the donation center. Dad may not be able to have Mom's stuff around, but I would go visit him just to be near her essence. I brought all her clothes, hats, perfume, coats, and shoes home. I needed more time with them. Over the next few weeks, I kept a couple of her fancy vintage hats and perfumes. The rest I brought to the Salvation Army.

Chapter Forty-Three

Barely six months after Mom passed, Dad called on a Saturday morning. "Can I come over for dinner tonight? Around four?

"Of course, Dad, see you then." He hung up, and I planned dinner for four at four.

Luke was mashing the potatoes when the doorbell rang. Jordan bounded off the couch to answer it. "Hi Grandpa." Then, "Oh, hi" he said again.

"Hello," a female voice said. I poked my head into the hall. My Mom's friend, Alice, who had been widowed two years ago, stood next to my dad.

"Hi guys," I said, abandoning the green beans and walking down the hall, wiping my hands on my apron. I welcomed them with hugs and said to Alice, "This is a surprise. Dad didn't tell me you were coming."

"I'm sorry, you know how he is." She smiled at him. "A man of few words."

I know that. Why are you smiling at my dad? I plastered my best polite smile across my face and took their jackets. "Dinner will be ready in a minute."

Lively chatter came from the living room. Jordan entertained them with karate moves. I returned to the green beans.

Luke came in and looked at me with his *how 'bout that* grin. He pointed behind him with his thumb. "Is this a date?" he asked in a hushed voice.

"I'm trying to pretend I'm dreaming," I whispered and scrunched my face. "He didn't even tell me she was coming."

Luke grabbed the oven mitts from the hook on the wall and took the ham out of the oven. He carved it and placed it on the platter I set out for him. Once the table was set, now with five plates, I called everyone in.

There was pleasant conversation at the table. We were in the middle of the apple pie Luke and Jordan made that morning when my father stood.

"I have something to tell all of you," he said and looked at Alice. "*We* have something to tell you." He took her hand.

My unblinking eyes darted to Luke and then back to my dad. A forkful of apple pie and ice cream hovered over my dessert plate.

"I know this will surprise all of you, but Alice and I have decided to get married."

"What?" I dropped my fork onto the plate and stood. My chair jutted out and hit the wall behind me. "How long have you two been together?" My eyes burned at Alice.

"Now just settle down, Missy," he said and held his hand up. "There was no funny business before your mom passed, if that is what you are asking. Alice and I started talking after your mother died. You know Alice's Daniel died two years ago." He took Alice's hand again. "She has helped me with a lot of hard emotions. We decided we care for each other and are too old to wait. We want to be married."

I fell back into my chair with my elbows on my knees and my face in my hands. Sobs that wouldn't stay put escaped my lips and tears fell through my fingers. I could feel Luke's giant hand on my back. My dad pulled his chair to sit in front of me.

"It's just a shock. I'm sorry." I managed as I put my arms around him. "I still cry for her every day." Other chairs slid across the linoleum and footsteps padded out of the kitchen. I didn't try to stop them.

"I should have approached things differently, sweetheart. Sorry for springing this on you," he said through emotion that threatened tears as well.

"It's too soon."

"I know you think so, but time is different when you are older. We want to have as much time together as possible."

I stayed there in his embrace. In those moments I realized my thoughts of, *How could you do this to Mom?* were really, how could you do this to *me*? This had nothing to do with me. This was what he needed. No one here was doing this to hurt me. It was what Dad was doing in his life to make it bearable for him.

We parted, and I kissed his cheek. "I love you. I want you to be happy."

I used my napkin to blot some of my tears and dried my face as best I could. One more hug around the neck and I took his hand and went to the living room with everyone else. Alice stood up as we came in and started to explain. I held up my hand. "I'm sorry I was so shocked in there. I understand now." I walked over and gave her a hug. The rest of the night, I sat on the couch next to her and laced her fingers with mine.

Two weeks later, I was hugging a stepmother.

Many mothers have passed through my life; a biological mother, older sisters who mothered me, The Ladies. Then Millie, my adopted mother, who truly loved me. Millie became the mother everyone should have. She showed me, through example, how to be a wife and, through advice and love, how to be a good person. Now Alice, my stepmother. She was very sweet, and I couldn't help but warm up to her when I saw how much she cared for my dad.

19 Years Ago

Chapter Forty-Four

I blinked and another five years flashed by. Julie married John in the spring of 1991 and moved to Oregon. Luke and I flew to Seattle for the wedding. They had their first baby, Gentle Jonny, a month ago.

Jen still lived and worked in Boston. Jen and James live on the same street, but not in the same apartment. He married a woman named Coco a year ago. Jen met Shar at their wedding and fell in love soon after. She brought Shar to meet us with Sweet Skye on spring break, and we instantly bonded. Shar was skinny as a rail, with pin straight jet black hair and wore her emotions on her sleeve.

Jess performed in play after play, loving every minute of living in New York City.

This year Jess was between plays, so she could come home for Christmas. Jen and Shar brought Sweet for a visit, too.

On December nineteenth, Paul, Luke's stepfather, called to say Elsa was in the hospital suffering from chest pain.

"The doctor said it was a heart attack. Paul says Mom is fine, but I'm going anyway. I'll just stay overnight." Luke said after he hung the receiver on the hook. He sat on the chair I kept by the phone.

I kissed his head and sat on his lap with my arms around his neck. "I'll come too."

"No, you stay here. You have work and the kids are visiting. Mom will be fine," he said, trying to believe it himself. "I just want to put my eyes on her."

"Okay, but you shouldn't put a time limit on it. Come back whenever you're ready." He hugged me tight and took a deep breath before getting up.

"I'm coming," Jess said. She hopped from the couch and went to pack an overnight bag. Luke shrugged at me and did the same. I was glad he wouldn't be alone.

I shoved some hastily made sandwiches into a paper sack as they both came into the kitchen to say goodbye. In a group hug, we all said goodbye, and Luke said a quick prayer for his mom. As we walked past the living room, the pink butterfly clock read a quarter past one.

I hugged and kissed them both again and waved from the door. I watched as they drove out of the driveway. Jordan bumped into me as he ran out to make a snowball to throw at their rear window. We laughed and waved as we watched them drive down the road and turn at the stop sign.

Later that night, Luke called me from his mom's place. "Hey babe. She's going to be alright. She's weak, but she'll recover. She was bummed about having to spend Christmas at the hospital, but Paul brought a small fake tree for her bedside table."

After two days, Luke and Jess decided to head home because there was a storm in the forecast. Luke called me at one o'clock before they left. "We'll be home for dinner. Make something good," he joked.

When six thirty rolled around, snow started to fall. I fed everyone and tried not to let on how worried I was. At seven thirty, a white blanket covered the roads. My heart jumped when the phone rang.

Please let it be them. My prayer went up. I picked up the receiver with my eyes squeezed shut and tried to make my heart believe it would be Luke or Jess on the other end.

"Hello?" It was neither. It was the hospital in Talaboo. They confirmed my fears and told me that there had been a car accident. They needed me to come right away.

"Okay, thank you. I'll be right there." I hung up but could not turn to face Jen and Shar seated at the table behind me. I rested my head on the yellow-coated wall beside the neon blue phone. Jen and Shar stood and put their arms around me when I told them.

"I'll stay and wait with Skye. You guys go," Shar said.

Jen hugged her and kissed her on the cheek. "You're the best," she said, tucking Shar's hair behind her ear.

Jen, Jordan, and I bundled up and started out for the hospital. Jen drove. The thirty minute drive took us double that because of the snow. Anxiety squeezed my chest, and I couldn't get a full breath for most of the ride.

Between the stress and the snow, everything seemed the way it does in a dream. You try to get somewhere, but you can never move fast enough. We arrived at the hospital at about a quarter past nine. The nurse at the front desk pointed out a police officer as he came to greet us.

"Thank you for coming, Mrs. Marcome. So sorry it had to be in this kind of weather. Please have a seat." He motioned to the avocado-green waiting room chairs. Jordan and Jen were on either side of me. I felt nauseous.

"Where are Luke and Jessica?"

"I'm sorry to tell you this, but your daughter was killed this afternoon in a car accident." He said more words, but I didn't hear them.

My baby daughter? Dead? "Where is my husband?" I tried to say, but I only got out, "Where…".

I had my own personal earthquake. Shaking so much I couldn't support my weight even sitting in these awful lime-green chairs. Everything went dark. The next thing I remember is waking up in a hospital bed with the kids next to me.

Jordan's eyes filled with tears. "I was so scared," he said and hugged me. "When you passed out, you fell off the chair. I thought you had died of a heart attack or something."

I had been out for ten minutes. "The doctor said you just fainted." Jen's voice came from behind him.

"Sorry honey," I said. Deciding to pretend the last fifteen minutes never happened because they were obviously a mistake, I said, "Where is Luke?"

I shewed away the nurse as she tried to tell me to stay in bed and pulled away the curtain. Jen led me to his room.

Patches of dried blood were clumped in his brown hair and the left side of his face was spotted black and blue. Bruises and bumps were all over his arms. The doctor came in and told us he had extensive internal injuries and the next twenty-four hours would be crucial to know if he was going to make it.

Make it. I said it over and over in my head. At first it started as a question: *Make it?* As in, *will he?* Then it became a plea. *Make it! Please, make it!*

With tears threatening to fall and a shaky voice, I stroked Luke's face and whispered close to his ear, "I love you. Jordan, Jen, and I will be right here sitting with you." He made no motion to let me know he heard or felt anything.

As snow fell outside, I waited by his bedside. I rested my head on the bed near his hand and fell asleep. I woke to Luke's hand on my head. I forgot where I was for a moment. Remembering, I stood to look into Luke's eyes. Jordan was beside me.

"Jen, can you get the nurse?" I asked through tears, never looking away from Luke.

He didn't say a word, he just looked at me with soft eyes and an almost smile. "You had us so scared," I said as I tried to touch him somewhere that wasn't hurt or bloody.

That one tender moment. That one sentence. Then Luke's eyes hazed and stared off at the corner of the room. Alarms started going off and there was a flutter of activity from the medical professionals. We were pressed out of the way and out of the room. A nurse tried to lead us down the hall away from Luke's room.

"I'm staying here," I cried out desperately as I clung to the threshold, only moving my hands when another nurse closed the door behind us.

"Ma'am, I need you to calm down and come to the waiting room." She reached out for my elbow.

"Don't you fucking touch me again." I ripped myself from her grasp. Hearing the drone of the flat line and the bang of the defibrillator, I covered my gaping mouth with my hands, hoping to cover the scream that threatened to escape. My eyes were as wide as possible, looking at the kids coming towards me. I held out my other hand for them to stay away. I backed up until I hit the wall and slid down until my knees were at my forehead. I hugged my legs, so my arms covered my ears. Jen and Jordan were now by my side. We cried together on the floor.

When the doctor came out of the room, we were still in our huddle. We heard all that happened, but he told us anyway. Then he said, "I'm sorry, Mrs. Marcome, we did everything we could."

Luke was gone. Luke was gone, Jess was gone, and I was left here screaming on ugly green tiles with Jen and Jordan the only things holding me together. Jen agreed with the doctor when he suggested a tranquilizer.

Medicated, my sobs ceased, but my sorrow didn't. I went into Luke's room. I brushed his hair off his face and kissed his cheek. The chair scraped across the floor as I moved it back into the place next to his bed. I put my head down and moved his large hand over my head. I stayed there silently, trying to turn back time, as my tears fell onto the mattress.

Laying there I felt a hand on my back. I turned to see Jordan. I touched his face. "I want to hug him. Is that weird?" Jordan asked.

"You should hug him if you want to honey," I said. "I will too." We both leaned in and hugged Luke. Jordan even climbed up and laid next to him. I don't know how long we were there before Jen came to get us.

Jen brought us to Jess, already in the morgue. Jordan stayed outside with Jen while I went in. Jess was battered and bruised as well, but more peaceful somehow. Maybe it was my tranquilizer. I stroked her hair and held her cold hand.

"Oh Jess," I said and kissed her forehead. I pulled up a chair and rested my elbow on the metal table she laid on. I sat there with my head in my hand and my other arm across her until Jen came in to guide me out.

Jen took over all the signing and organizing that had to do with my daughter and husband. When the snow stopped at about five in the morning. Jen drove us all home. Like a zombie, I let her lead me to my bedroom and help me into my pajamas. Covering me like I used to do for her when she was young, she smoothed my hair out of my face and kissed my cheek.

"I'm so sorry Ma. Try to get some rest." She turned with damp eyes and walked out, leaving the door ajar.

At lunch time, I hauled myself out of bed and got some water from the kitchen sink. I leaned on the counter with my free hand and saw three fuzzy figures sitting at the table. "Where's Jordan?" My heart skipped a beat, realizing I was so out of it when we left the hospital. I don't even remember if he was in the car on the way home.

"He went to David's house after breakfast. Should I call him back?" Jen stood.

"No, no, sit down. It's okay. He needs his friends right now."

Everyone got clearer as my eyes focused. I sat at the table and Shar brought me some tea.

"I'm sorry Nanna," said Sweet Skye. Her little arms came in for a hug. Tears filled but didn't escape my eyes. I hugged her back and thanked her.

I looked past Jen to the couch. Less than twenty-four hours ago, I set things out for Jess to sleep on the couch, the same as she had been doing for three nights before she left with Luke.

"I put the bedding back in the closet. I hope that was okay," Jen said.

"Thank you honey," I said absently.

"I called and told some people. I hope that was okay, too."

"Yes, thank you again. I was not up for that. Who did you call?"

"Well, I called Julie, and Aunt Patty. Some of Jess's friends I knew of, and Luke's work." Jen looked at me to see if I was okay. "Julie is getting a plane ticket as we speak. Is there anyone else you wanted me to call? I didn't know if you wanted to call anyone yourself."

"I'll call Paul and Grandpa." I told her in a weak voice. I brought the phone to my ear but could only sit and listen to the dial tone. I hung it back on its hook when the warning tone came over the receiver.

I turned to them. "Maybe you could call them." I pleaded with my eyes. "And anyone else you could think of." Jen nodded her head. "I think I need to go back and lie down for a bit. Tell me when Jordan is home, okay?"

"No problem," Jen said.

I didn't go to my room. I walked to the closet, opened the door, and reached for the pillow Jess slept on when she was here. I pulled it down from the shelf, held it close, and inhaled deeply.

The scent filled my head with memories of my daughter. Baby Jess. Teen Jess. Grown-up Jess on her way to New York with Patti.

My mind turned to the memories I would never have. She had dreams of being a movie actress, director, and producer. She wanted to be a wife and a mother. All those memories were taken from me. I closed myself into the closet and sank to the floor. I dozed off next to the vacuum, hugging Jess's pillow.

I woke up when I heard Jen calling for me. Feeling a little embarrassed, I opened the door. "Here," I said.

"Ma?" she asked. "What's going on?"

"I just wanted to be close to her." I barely got the words out before tears overcame me. Jen came down and hugged me. We cried together on the closet floor. She helped me up and put me back into bed.

Back in my room alone, I lay on my side of the bed, half covered while I stared at Luke's side. I reached across and spread my hand wide on his empty spot. I walk my fingers over his pillow where his head should be. *Are you here? Do you see me? Are you touching my head, trying to comfort me?* I touch my head and try to feel his hand. *I feel you here, in everything.*

Tears crossed the bridge of my nose. "How can you be gone when your scent still fills my head?" I said to his cold pillow. I pulled it close to me and squeezed it tight. *Maybe hugging this hard enough will force you back into existence.*

I whispered, "Maybe I'll open my eyes and there you will be, telling me how this is all a horrible dream and Jess is asleep on the couch." I opened my eyes to find only the pillow. In the silence, I cried myself to sleep.

Jen came into the bedroom at about six that evening. Waking me, she told me Jordan had been home since three. She lay on the bed next to me, face to face.

"Mom, do you want to hear what the officer told me about what happened?"

After a long pause, I nodded my head. She started quietly, as if that would make it hurt less.

"Even though Luke and Jess called at one, they didn't start out until three, and it was getting dark fast because the storm was coming in. There was no snow on the roads yet. Jess was driving in the fast lane. The officer said she was possibly speeding a bit, but not much. Another car going well over the speed limit came up on them fast on route ninety. As the other car tried to pass them on the right, it clipped Jess's bumper."

Jen stopped talking and rolled onto her back. Staring at the ceiling, she went on. "Jess lost control, and it sent her into the guardrail. She died instantly, but Luke was brought to the hospital. The driver of the other car spun out of control, rolled his car three times, and was also pronounced dead at the scene. No other cars were hit."

I didn't respond. I only took in the information. After we laid there together for a bit, I made a head motion that suggested we should get up and go into the kitchen.

At the table, we worked out the details of the memorial services. Jen and Shar helped me through every detail. We decided it was best to have a wake for them on December twenty-seventh.

In the days that followed, I had nothing but questions for God through my tears and tranquilizers. *I thought you gave him to me.* I called out, wet-faced to the ceiling many times a day. *How could you take my baby girl?* Tissues were spread everywhere.

Julie and John came in with Gentle Jonny. I held and loved him from the moment they got there. Jordan gave up his room and slept on the couch or curled up in a ball at the end of my bed.

Chapter Forty-Five

I was in the middle of Jess's eulogy when someone slipped into the back of the room. He tried to come in quietly. When I saw him, I fell silent, trying to decide what to do next.

He wore a black suit and tie and a solemn expression. His blonde hair was combed back. His blue eyes were dulled by age and grief. Matt.

I didn't even think of him in these past few days. *How could you come?*

The girls followed my gaze. Julie gasped and whispered to John, "I didn't think my dad would come." Then everyone turned to see him.

"Holy shit," Shar said. She grabbed Jen's hand and held it to her chest.

"I shouldn't have come." He held up his hands and turned to leave.

His hand was on the door when I found my voice. "You can stay," I said louder than I meant to. All eyes were volleying from me to him.

He turned back with the weight of everyone's eyes. "I'm sorry. I don't want to cause any trouble. Laura called, and I had to come."

I walked out from behind the podium to him and took his hand. "You should be here. She was your daughter."

"Look," he said, "You don't have to do this."

I looked into his eyes. "I don't do anything that I don't want to do anymore, Matt. Now, come in before my kindness runs out and say hello to your children and grandchildren."

His eyes opened wide and looked over my shoulder to see a grown Julie and Jen with their families beside them.

"That is my Jordan next to them in blue," I said.

"He looks just like Luke."

"I know." Tears escaped through my smile when I blinked. I walked him over to them, pretending no one was watching.

After a minute, I turned to everyone there. "Everyone here knew Luke and Jess. You know neither of them would want us crying and moaning over them or excluding anyone from being here. They would want us to be happily retelling wonderful stories about them and laughing at the times we had together. Please get up and mingle and share anything that comes to mind."

Chapter Forty-Six

Julie and her family had to leave a day after the memorial. Jen, Shar, and Sweet had to head home the day after that. They all had work and school.

Just like that, Jordan and I were alone. Work told me to take as much time as I needed.

Once all the guests were gone and Jordan was back at school, the loneliness of my empty home was unbearable. I just lay in bed all day. Most days I talked to the room as if talking to God, or Luke, or Jess, hoping for some sort of response.

My friend, Nancy, would visit often. Usually she would come and lie with me or sit on the armchair near the window and read. She lost her husband three years ago, a year before we met.

Jordan had been back to school two weeks, so it had to be mid-January. Today Nancy sat on the floor near my bed, staring at the wall for thirty minutes.

"You know I love you like a sister." She turned her head to face me. "I know you are hurting, losing Luke and Jess came out of nowhere. "

"Just tell me this will stop hurting someday," I said through my tissue.

"It will never stop hurting." She was looking right into my eyes. "You will always remember this with pain. You'll remember every single solitary second from the time he left for his mom's to the second you left the hospital."

I turned away from her. She came to the other side of the bed to see my face again and went on. "You'll go over it and over it, wondering what could have happened differently. For a while, that's all you'll remember."

Taking a deep breath, she laid on the bed with me and continued, "Unfortunately, time doesn't stop, and people here need you. So try to think about how you can help them. Through them, each day will seem a little less painful. Through them, the sun will peak in just a little more. Tragedy will always come, but so will joy, if you let it."

Oof, like a punch to the gut, she was right.

"Someday," Sandy said, "you'll not think about the hospital so much, but you'll be able to remember the good times. The other unexpected times with good outcomes. Someday, remembering their love won't hurt so much. Someday it may make you happy," she said.

I wept hard tears and Nancy held me the whole time.

When all my tears were cried out and my face looked like a marshmallow, I composed myself. I pulled away from Nancy and thanked her. "I think I'll go take a shower," I said.

"Thank God!"

A laugh escaped me, and I covered my face.

"It's okay, you're going to be okay." She hugged me one more time and then helped me out of bed.

Taking a shower was a cleansing for my soul. As the water washed over me, my strength returned. When I came out into the kitchen, Nancy had gone home, but Jordan sat at the oak dining table with his schoolbooks open. I sat down with him.

"Can I get you some tea, mom?" He was up and at the kettle before I answered. "I'm glad you're out of bed."

"Sorry I've been down so long. I wish I could've been better for you," I said, tears welling up.

"Don't worry," he said. "I've been sad, but it's okay. I was just happy you were here." The words caught in his throat a bit. "It has been so lonely without dad. It was nice to go in and stay with you."

He put my tea in front of me and hugged my shoulders. "I think about Jess sometimes too," he continued. "It's harder to miss her as much as Dad because she's been gone for so long. It just seems like she's back there, ya know, in New York. Then I remember," he said as his eyes filled up.

I stood and hugged him, and we both cried for a minute.

"I'm still not ready to face the world," I told him. "Can we sit and watch something on TV?" He nodded his head and wiped his eyes. He set us up on the couch with a blanket to share.

We ordered pizza and sat there and watched for hours. I woke up in the night, still there on the couch. I watched the rise and fall of Jordan's chest. I studied the lines of his ever changing preteen face and said a thankful prayer because he was still here. I fell back to sleep with his head on my shoulder.

Our wedding anniversary and Valentine's Day passed. Nancy was over most days after Jordan and her daughter, Sandy, went to school. I made tea and Nancy set out the homemade cupcakes she brought. I filled the hole in my heart with delicious frosting and spongy goodness. It seemed like food was my only comfort since the accident.

11 Years Ago

Chapter Forty-Seven

I was once again at my clinic with a UTI.

"I'm going to send you for some extra tests," the doctor said. "I'd like to know more clearly what is going on with your bladder and kidneys." X-rays, an ultrasound, and a few blood tests later, I was in the office again to hear my results.

After telling me there was a mass in one of my kidneys, he told me about Dr. Brook-Allen, an oncologist. He already made an appointment for me to see her on Tuesday morning next week.

"I'm coming with you," Jordan said over his cereal when I told him Monday morning.

"No, I'll be fine. There is nothing to worry about," I said, even though I didn't believe the words.

"I am coming with you," he said.

I knew there was no swaying him. He was a senior and had no morning classes. I could use the feeling of ease he brought to all situations, the same as Luke. I gave in.

The following Tuesday, we sat in the pale blue waiting room. The television was too loud, and the receptionist was too chipper.

"Mrs. Marcome?" The nurse looked around the room for recognition. She met my eyes and escorted us back to Dr. Brook-Allen's office.

We all sat there in silence. I was surprised I couldn't hear the television on the wall in the waiting room. It seemed too loud when we were in there. I wondered if the television's volume and the placement of the doctor's office, down the hall and around the corner, were that way on purpose. How many people flipped out when they were told?

Cancer? Is that what she said?

I couldn't even pronounce the type of cancer yet. Was it curable? Am I dead? The only thing I knew was that the lovely, young, blond doctor said "Malignant". Even though it was not her fault, I hated her at that moment.

Jordan and the doctor were in the office with me, but I felt completely alone.

I wanted to go back ten minutes when I was tapping my nails again and again on the arm of my chair. Jordan joked we should make a break for it and go to breakfast instead. I wish we had.

ccRCC.

"A lot of letters, I know. It's Clear Cell Renal Cell Carcinoma," said Dr. Megan Brook-Allen again and looked at me for recognition. When she didn't get it, she turned to Jordan. He recorded the information in a notebook he brought.

"She has a mass on her right kidney, and we will have to remove it. The whole kidney, not only the mass." She said to Jordan. She really was doing her best to be informative and clear, but none of it was getting through to me.

Thank God for Jordan. He wrote everything down and was very good at asking her questions: How long before the surgery? What is to be done after? Will there be Chemo?

Dr. Brook-Allen gave him all the answers. Then he asked the question that brought me back to the room, "How long can she live with this sort of cancer?"

"At this time, I can't say. With your mother's other health concerns, the best course of action is to get that kidney out and go from there."

"I want a second opinion," I choked out. I took a sip from the water bottle I brought everywhere. "Is that something that can happen first?"

"Of course, but please do that quickly. The faster we get to this, the clearer the picture will be as to your future."

Okay, I thought, *second opinion. Hope. Future.*

Two weeks later, I was at Dr. James Blake's office. "Please have a seat," he said, motioning to the padded wooden chair across from his desk. I came alone this time.

A middle-aged man who looked over the tests that Dr. Brook-Allen had sent, as well as the new ones he ordered last week.

"How do they look? Is it bad?" I asked.

I hoped he would jump up and holler, "It was all a mistake, Hallelujah!" No such luck.

He looked at me with a furrowed brow and said, "Mrs. Marcome, I am sorry, but it is ccRCC. You will have to have your kidney removed. And it needs to be soon. Should I schedule it, or would you like the original doctor to take it?" The words hung there for a moment. They kept echoing in my head, *original doctor, take it, removed, soon, removed.*

I felt like I was going to be sick.

Later that night, "Pass the corn, please?" I asked.

Jordan passed the bowl, and I scooped a pile of loose kernels onto my plate. He had no idea that I had gone to the doctor's that day. "How was school?"

"It was okay. I'll be happy in a few months once graduation is over. Everyone is pretty crazy with prom fever."

Having to put this burden on him at this time of his life broke my heart. With so many years between him and the girls, it was almost like he was an only child. He has had to deal with all my health issues, even from the start of his life.

He deserved to know. "Jordan, I got the second opinion today."

He looked up with a start. "Why did you go without me? I always want to know what is going on with you."

"I know, and thank you, but I had a feeling there would not be any new information." Looking into Jordan's hopeful eyes, I said, "And there wasn't. He said that Dr. Brook-Allen was right. The only thing to decide is which doctor will take out my kidney."

Chapter Forty-Eight

Dr. Brook-Allen scheduled the surgery two weeks away. I used those two weeks to put meals in the freezer and stock up on everyday stuff.

The morning of the surgery, dread held my chest tight and my stomach in knots. Nancy and Sandy brought us in. Jordan was holding my hand as Sandy, who was also Jordan's girlfriend, opened the door for us.

"Elizabeth Marcome, here for surgery," I said to the receptionist at the semi-circle desk in the hospital's lobby. She looked at her computer screen and motioned for us to have a seat. Others were waiting as well. Everyone looked as uncomfortable as us.

It wasn't long before a nurse made her way down the hall and greeted us. "Elizabeth?" she asked and looked between Nancy and me.

"That would be me," I said.

"Follow me," she said as she turned and started walking.

Everyone stood and followed. Turning, the nurse held her palm out, "Only one person can come with her right now. Others can wait here or come back and visit later."

Nancy and Sandy hugged me and told Jordan they would wait in the lobby. "We'll see you soon." She pointed at me and then walked back to the waiting area with Sandy. Ms. Nurse, Jordan, and I continued down the hallway.

I got undressed behind the flimsy hospital curtain and put on the flimsy hospital gown. I hopped up on my bed and Ms. Nurse set me up with an IV. After that, everything was wonderful. The calming drugs that were added to the IV line made me a little loopy. "After these messages, I'll be right back," I sang to Jordan, joking about a phrase from an old cartoon.

"I will be here," he said. It reminded me of Luke.

In the operating room, there was the normal hustle and bustle as they got ready to cut someone open. The anesthesiologist covered my face with a plastic cup and had me count backward. Ten…nine…eight…

I woke up and I looked around my room. Sandy sat on the chair by the window. Jordan stood behind her, looking down into the courtyard, hands in his pockets, as always. Sandy has been Jordan's girlfriend since tenth grade. She was blonde and slim like Nancy, and so kind.

"Can you get the nurse?" Jordan asked Sandy when they noticed my eyes were open. Her purple dress swished on the way out.

"How do you feel?" he asked.

"A little groggy and nauseous, but I'll be okay." I sounded weaker than I wanted to. "How did things go? Did they take the kidney? Did the doctor talk to you?"

"Yes, and things mostly went according to plan." He looked at the door, waiting for the nurse. When she wasn't there after a second, he added, "Your blood pressure tanked, and they almost lost you. They had to shock your heart."

I called Julie and Jen that evening to tell them I felt alright. I stayed in the hospital for a few days and then went home and recovered in my own bed.

Chapter Forty-Nine

Anything I asked, Jordan did without complaint. He had a peaceful, giving spirit he got from his father.

Three weeks passed without a hitch, and I got cleared to resume regular easy activity. Just in time for graduation.

At Jordan's high school graduation, I sat there with the other parents at the ceremony. My heart was racing. I raised my hand and sent a wave to Nancy three rows down. Nancy had remarried two years ago and now held tight to her husband's arm.

The lights went dim, and the presenters started the ceremony. My claustrophobia kicked in, but I pushed it down. *I'm in a big space,* I told myself. *Darkness is not solid. I can see the stage. I'm in an open place.* The words repeated in my head as I tried to listen to the Valedictorian.

Once the seniors started coming forward for their diplomas, there was more to focus on. I waited and clapped politely while waiting for them to call Jordan's name.

There was Sandy. I clapped wildly. Jordan was coming soon. Tears came down my cheeks.

"Jordan Marcome," the announcer called out. I whooped and snapped as many pictures as I could of his tiny figure walking across the stage. As he walked offstage, I sat down. A wave of tiredness came over me. There was still half a class left to get diplomas, but I walked up the aisle and stepped outside.

A wave of cool air hit my face as I pushed the heavy auditorium door open. I sat on some seats set up against the wall and took some deep breaths. I closed my eyes and rested the back of my head against the wall. I could hear people moving and chatting down the hall. A moment or two went by when I heard a voice that seemed to be talking to me.

"Excuse me, are you okay?" I opened my eyes and saw a man. He was wearing a superman blue button down and a black tie. His long dark dreads were neatly tied back with a thick cord.

"Yes, thank you," I said, feeling a little embarrassed. "I just got a little overwhelmed inside." My eyes flitted to the arena doors.

"I understand that." His smile drew in a deep dimple on his left cheek. "After my first born walked across the stage, I came out here for some air too."

"How nice, my youngest just did. Last of four," I said. "What is your child's name?"

"Keisha Carpenter. My name is Samuel. You?" he said as he stuck out his hand.

I took his hand in a friendly shake. "My son is Jordan, I'm Beth Marcome.

We sat and talked while the rest of the graduating class got their diplomas. I stood up as everyone filed out, signifying the end of the ceremony.

"Can I buy you a coffee sometime?" Samuel asked.

I hadn't been on a date since Luke passed. I think Samuel mistook my stunned silence for disinterest.

"I'm sorry, that was too forward, wasn't it? Or wait, are you married. I didn't see a ring, so…"

I shook my head back to the moment. "No, sorry. It wasn't too forward. You're right, I'm not married either. I just haven't been asked out in a while." I smiled and shook my head again. "Coffee sounds great." I gave him my phone number, and he texted his right back.

Chapter Fifty

One week later, I sat again with the doctor; she told me there wasn't much else the doctors could do at this point. They extracted the kidney and with it, the tumor. There were, what Dr. Brook-Allen called, routine blood tests. With my heart condition so far advanced at this point, there weren't any medicines or therapies that would be a benefit.

"As far as we know right now, we've got all the cancer. In a couple of months, I need you to come back for a chest x-ray, just as a precaution. The one before the surgery was clear. Clear lungs are a good sign that the cancer has not spread, which means we've halted the cancer at stage two." Dr. Brook-Allen stood and stuck out her hand. Realizing she was ending the appointment, I shook her hand and left.

Over the next couple of weeks, I had coffee with Samuel three times. He was a sixty-year-old divorced plumber and had custody of his three children. Keisha just graduated with Jordan, Kenya will be a senior next year and Sam Jr. will be a freshman.

I told him how I had been married twice; divorced, then widowed. I told him about Julie, Jen, Jess, and Jordan. He said I had a thing for J's, and I didn't disagree. His hand came to my arm when I spoke of Luke and Jess. The pain wasn't sharp enough to sting my eyes anymore, but it was there.

Jordan thought Samuel and I were cute. "I love that you're dating, Mom."

"This isn't dating, it's coffee," I said, trying to believe that myself.

"Whatever you say," he replied, holding up his hands. "Just so you know, I think he is a good guy, and I wouldn't mind you dating him sometime."

"You think so?"

"Ya, Keisha is pretty nice. I had a couple of classes with her. She seems to have her head on straight." He put his head down, interested in his spaghetti. "Good kids, good parents, right?"

Surprised by what I realized was a compliment to me, I replied, "Well that's usually true," I tried to hide my smirk as he looked through his peripheral to see if I caught his meaning.

August fifteenth, back to the hospital for my routine x-ray. Two days later, Jordan and I were in her office. Again, it was a comfort to have him. Again, it was bad news.

Dr. Brook-Allen let out a sigh. "You have two spots on your lungs that were not there before the surgery."

My knuckles were white as I gripped the arms of the chair, but I said nothing.

"What does that mean?" Jordan asked.

"It means your mom's cancer must have spread just before we took the kidney. Her lungs were clear three days before the surgery. It is unusual, but it happens. Instead of stage two, you have gone into stage four cancer. I'm so sorry Beth," she said.

She said there isn't much that can be done about this type of cancer. "The traditional procedures such as Chemo or Immunotherapy aren't possible with your heart problems. We can only monitor it. X-rays and pet scans will help us know how quickly your symptoms will progress."

"Are you telling me I'm dying?" I asked, slumping further into her uncomfortable seats.

"I am telling you, Mrs. Marcome, that your cancer is stage four. End stage," she said and glanced at my files again. "There is no telling how quickly or slowly the cancer will progress from here."

I heard her go on, but couldn't process her words. *End stage* was on repeat in my thoughts. Poor Jordan, how awful. He is barely nineteen.

When we got home, Jordan sat on the couch. I sat next to him and put my arm around him. "What's going on in there?" I asked, ruffling his hair.

He looked at me, "I've always thought I would lose you in an instant to a heart attack," he said with a blank face. "Not sick with cancer. It doesn't seem fair. You've already had too much pain."

I took a slow, deep breath. "No one should expect fairness when it comes to life or death," I said. "When we die is not usually up to us. We have to choose to make it through life in the best way we can."

"Nana, Jess, and Dad were all taken so quickly. Without any warning. I hate knowing you'll be sick here while I'm at school." He looked out the window. "Maybe I should stay home."

"The hell you will," I almost shouted as I stood. "This situation will not stop your future. I have people here to help me if I need it," I said, sitting back down. "I may have six months or ten years. I could never be happy with one minute I have left if I thought I was hurting your future." I linked my arm into his. "You won't be far and can come back if you feel you need to if something happens to me."

"Okay mom, but I'm scared," he said and hugged me. I could feel his tears on my shoulder. "You have to promise to be honest with me about any information you get. Also, call me if there is any change in your health."

"I can do that." I said. *I'm scared too.* I wanted to tell him, but instead we sat quietly on the couch there for most of the morning. It was eleven o'clock when I got up and made lunch, pretending it was any other day.

Chapter Fifty-One

This is the first time I've met with Samuel for coffee since my doctor's appointment. He knew about my health problems, but not the stage four diagnosis.

"It's been nice getting to know you, but I don't want to date or become close to anyone. I hope you understand."

He smiled an easy smile. "Not really. I've enjoyed getting to know you. There's no pressure here."

Stealing myself, I said, "I don't think we should meet for coffee anymore. This is the last time I'll come out."

"Hey now, that isn't necessary," he said, reaching out to touch my arm.

"Maybe it isn't, but it's how I want it." I stood to leave. "It was nice getting to know you. I wish you well."

"Where's this coming from? You've become a really great friend."

"I've gotten a new diagnosis. I'm in stage four." My eyes welled up. I cursed myself and sat back in my seat.

He dragged his cafe chair closer to me. "You must be terrified," he said, putting his arm around me.

A few sobs escaped before I could stop them. I nestled into his chest for a moment. Then I remembered why I came out to meet him today.

I stood, "I apologize. We can't see each other anymore. We can't be friends either. I've grown to care for you, and I couldn't be just a friend while you date someone else." I turned and left him there at the outdoor table of the cafe.

Catching up to me, he caught me up in a kiss. My eyes closed in surrender for a moment. Then, seeing the future of him watching me die, I pulled away.

"I'm sorry. Please don't call me."

In my car, the slightest tinge of regret crept in. A few tears slipped from my eyes. *He deserved to find someone he could love. Someone that he would have the potential to grow into old age with. Not a ticking time bomb.*

9 Years Ago

Chapter Fifty-Two

Three x-rays and two PET scans later showed the tumors had stalled. In fact, there was an actual mistake on the original x-ray. There were still two spots, but instead of one spot at nine millimeters and one spot at two millimeters as I was told in the beginning, it was actually a six and a two-millimeter spot. Both the tumors went to three millimeters and stayed there. Yes, one shrunk on its own.

Today at my appointment, Dr. Brook-Allen called it remission, kind of like a pause, but it could start progressing anytime. I called it an answer to prayers.

7 Years Ago

Chapter Fifty-Three

Still in remission, my heart gave me some trouble through the years. I developed congestive heart failure and was in and out of the hospital. I was put on even more medications and restrictive exercise. My weight went up, which made things worse.

5 Years Ago

Chapter Fifty-Four

"I don't want to give up my car," I said, red faced. The tips of my ears tingled as I tried hard to stay calm.

Jordan and Sandy sat at my kitchen table having tea while trying to convince me to give up my last hold on freedom.

"I only drive myself to church and doctor's appointments. How will I get around?"

"You know there are people at church that would be happy to pick you up," Jordan said.

"Also, my mom can help and there are rideshares or taxis that can take you to the doctors," Sandy said. "Mom says she loves it when you two go shopping together,"

"We just don't want you to get hurt." Jordan touched my arm.

They had good reason for concern. I've had two accidents in the last month. Actually, there'd been three. I didn't tell anyone I backed into a big red Target ball two weeks ago. It broke the taillight of my car. I drove straight to the auto repair place to have it fixed.

None of the accidents had injured anyone, but they were getting more frequent. The new pain medicine they had me on for my back made me more impaired than I wanted to admit.

"Can I say I'll think about it?"

All I have been doing is thinking about it. Between the fall I had three months ago and these accidents, all I could do was watch my independence slip from my grasp.

Two months and another accident later made me realize it was time. No more driving. I sold my car to the guy around the corner and sighed every time I saw him drive by.

I let Pastor Ann know about my need for a ride and soon I had three different offers. We've been loved and accepted since the first Sunday.

Pastor Ann also let the congregation know that I was homebound, and many people came to visit.

Being a shut-in wasn't so bad. The nurses and physical therapist came to you if you needed it.

Jordan was right. If I ever wanted to go somewhere, I just had to ask someone or call a taxi.

You count time differently when you are home all day long. You get up and go to bed whenever the heck you want, General Hospital and Wheel of Fortune dictate lunch and dinner.

7 Months Ago

Chapter Fifty-Five

Jen and Shar sat on my couch and told me Shar was two months pregnant.

"You're kidding? Amazing!" tears coming down my face, I fought to get out of my chair to hug them, but they came to me first. "That was the last thing I expected you guys to say."

"Shar really felt the urge to have a baby, so we made that happen." Jen said in the beaming mama way.

And then, knowing them well enough to ask, "How? Was it a friend, or a donor?" and then with raised eyebrows and tilted chin, "A stranger?"

They laughed at the last one. "It was a donor." They sat again and Jen took Shar's hand. "We decided because of Shar's Japanese heritage, we wanted to have a Japanese donor. So that's the way we went and

BAM pregnant. First try." Jen moved slightly to bump Shar's shoulder with hers. "We're going to be moms again," she said with the proudest of smiles.

They stayed overnight and drove back to Chicago in the morning.

4 Months Ago

Chapter Fifty-Six

Patty and Betty came to make me a tomato sauce as I sat at the kitchen table and chatted with them. Over the years, they have become like the same person, like any married couple that goes the distance. They have been together since they ran away to New York at seventeen years old, getting married officially as soon as Obama said they could.

They know where everything is in my house better than I do and talk to each other in a kind of shorthand language developed by years of practice. Both turned towards the stove. Betty hummed a sweet tune. Patty ran her hand down her love's back and swayed with her head on Betty's shoulder.

"Emily's just about to pop," I said. "I saw her on Skype the other day. She's getting uncomfortable."

"Yes." They both turn together. Patty came to the table. "That little baby is going to be so cute. Emily and John are gorgeous." She sat and fanned herself with a mail flier. "I was shocked when they got married so young. You don't see that much anymore."

"I was too, right out of high school," I put in. "They weren't even pregnant then." I laughed. "I can't wait to see that squishy little thing." I hugged my shoulders. "I hope they can make the trip with Julie and everyone. Gentle John was my second grandbaby. Now he and Emily are having my first great-grand-baby." I closed my eyes to hold back the tears that filled them.

Patty took my hand and kissed the back of it. We all know that there is no guarantee that I'll live to see the new babies.

"Have you seen Shar lately?" Betty asked, tossing some extra basil into the pot. "Oh my goodness, her little baby bump is the cutest thing. Can you believe she is doing this at forty-one?"

"Lots of women are waiting until their forties these days," Patty said.

"Will you be able to make the trip in June when everyone comes?" I asked. "Jordan and Sandy are staying with Nancy, but everyone else is cramming in here."

"Probably," Patty said, "We'll know better as things get closer. I'll be in rehearsals for *Standing* then. I may not be able to get away." *Standing* was a play Patty wrote about the hilarious plight of aging.

"The Astor theater will be fluttering with activity," Betty said as Patty got up to start the pasta. "It's perfect. A beautiful old theater for a play about a beautiful old woman." She turned and kissed Patty's cheek.

The whole house smelled of sausage, tomatoes, and herbs. I hadn't eaten yet and my head swam with the sensation of dipping crusty bread deep into the red liquid, sopping up every last drop. Plunging my fork deep into the pile of sausages and devouring the whole plate, along with a giant bowl of spaghetti.

Alas, that's not something I can do, not if I want to continue to breathe as long as possible. I took my small portion of pasta, with a half a slice of low sodium sandwich bread to sop up my moderate amount of sauce and one very, very small piece of sausage.

12 Days Ago

Chapter Fifty-Seven

Once they turned my IDC off at the hospital, they said I could go home.

Nancy brought me home and stayed to make dinner. I'm grateful for her help and friendship. There is, however, the tiniest part of me that's jealous if I think about it too long.

We're the same age. Sixty-six.

She doesn't look a day over fifty and bounces around here cleaning and cooking on those perfectly working legs. Meanwhile, I sit here and dread the time I'll have to make myself stand and navigate the walker down the hall. Even with the assistance of the self-raising armchair, it's a difficult task. My knees threaten to betray me at any moment. One more fall and they won't let me live alone.

11 Days Ago

Chapter Fifty-Eight

I rolled my walker out of the bathroom feeling pretty happy I made it in time, when the front door burst open. A four-legged Diego trotted in, followed by Jordan. Diego knew not to jump on me, but he got as close as possible and sat in the hall by my side.

"Good boy," I said, which made his tail sweep my floor. I pulled off a quick pat to his head before I needed my hand back on the walker.

Jordan and Sandy have been married for five years now. They haven't had any children, but they have given me a grand puppy in Diego, the amazing Goldendoodle.

"Hey Baby," I said as I one-arm-hugged Jordan, my other hand having a death grip on the walker. "What are you doing here?"

"Hi Ma," he said with his bear hug. "I had the day off and Diego wanted to come and say hi."

"Oh, *Diego* did?" Careful steps took me back to my seat. Diego found his favorite place by my side. "It's good to see you, too." I moved my hand to the furry head of my grand-dog and began my petting duties.

"Yes, he was hoping you would come to the park with us. It's still cool out. What do you think?" I knew what he was trying to do. The physical therapist told him I should move around more.

"Hmmm," I said while I tried to find an excuse. "Maybe the backyard. I'll walk on the grass, and you could throw the ball for Diego."

"What do you think?" Jordan looked at Diego for confirmation. "We accept."

At the back door was where I needed help. I held Jordan's forearms for support and forced my knee to raise my foot over the threshold down the half step to the deck. Off the deck, there was a nice patch of grass that Jordan mowed last Saturday.

Jordan walked backward with me still holding his arms. As we neared the steps, I grabbed the railing and moved my hand to Jordan's shoulder. We made it down the three steps without incident. After retrieving the walker from the hall, he tossed the ball to Diego.

As I recovered, sitting on the walker's seat, I took in the morning's beauty. It wasn't a giant yard, but Jordan tossed the ball and Diego was happy enough to bounce across the damp grass to chase it.

I closed my eyes and listened. "Good boy," he whispered to the pup. The birds talked to each other as they looked for breakfast and the cicadas hummed, telling us to get ready for a hot one.

"Do you want help around the yard?" Jordan asked.

I opened my eyes. "No, I'll try with just the walker." I took the handles and started out. I got down one side of the yard and turned back. "That is about all I can do today. I must still be tired from the trip home yesterday."

"That was a good effort," he said.

"Can you help me back into the air conditioning?"

"Of course," he said and tossed my walker over his shoulder. We got up the stairs and back to my chair without a problem. Diego followed us the whole way.

"How's Sandy?" I asked, trying to think of anything but my pounding heart and heaving lungs.

"She's good" He paused with a big smile on his face and seemed like he was going to tell me something. But instead he sat back and said, "She is excited to see everyone next week. We both are."

Happiness spread across my face at the thought of seeing all my children and grandchildren. "So am I. Having everyone here will be amazing." Then, the smallest microsecond of sadness came when the sting reminded me everyone would not be there.

"I know. It still stings for a second when I think of them too," Jordan said, taking my hand. He could always read my thoughts.

I kiss the back of his hand and put it on my cheek for a second. "Want to stay for a movie?"

"Sure. How about Bridgette Jones?"

"You know me well."

After the movie, Jordan made us some chicken soup with the no-salt broth Nancy left yesterday. The low-salt nature of my diet made the flavor of everything I ate these days muted.

Today he put in fresh herbs, and it really made a difference. Jordan was a great cook. I always thought he would be a chef. I was surprised when he and Sandy both went into software design. More money and less stress were his reasons.

After lunch, he and Diego said goodbye. He knew my soaps would start soon and Jim, my physical therapist, would be here at about four. Then to finish out the night, Julie would make her daily Facetime call about five.

"Tell Jim I already worked you out today."

"You bet I will. Maybe he will go easy on me."

"Doubt it," he smiled.

"Me too. I'll be in bed early tonight," I said as I stood to hug him and thank him for the day. "Lock the door on your way out, please."

"Why? Everyone knows you have a key in the mailbox." We both laughed because it was true. "I'll lock it, anyway."

"Thanks Baby," I said as he closed the door.

Alone again, I shut my eyes for a catnap.

9 Days Ago

Chapter Fifty-Nine

"Hey little Softie." I said into my phone screen. "Aren't you just the sweetest little thing?" Julie was holding the phone up to Softie Sophia, my first great-grandchild. She was squirming in her pink onesie that had a skirt sewn around the body. "You finally have a little girl, even if it's a grandchild."

"Everything will be pink!" Julie said with a flourish of her hand across the screen. She gave Softie a little tummy tickle.

The baby was three months old and had those amazing belly laughs no one could ignore and babbled out sounds that made you hear words when there were none. Today she was telling me all about how much she loved the taste of her fingers.

"That's right, Softie, you bring everyone with you next week when you come. Don't forget anyone."

"We're all excited too, Ma." Julie turned the screen to her. She had no makeup on, and her blonde hair was in a messy bun.

"You look tired. Are you okay?"

"Yes," she said and smoothed her hair back. "Just tired. How did you ever deal with us bringing every kid in the neighborhood home all the time?" She laughed off the stress with an eye roll. The youngest of her three boys and his two friends ran through the kitchen, as if on cue.

She has so many of Matt's features; blonde hair, blue eyes, cleft chin, high cheekbones, even his slender frame. She looked just like Laura. "How's your father?"

"He's fine. He retired a few months ago, except for tax season. He says he'll still go in for that to help out."

"Good. I'm glad," I said with all truthfulness. I forgave him long ago. Life is too short to hold on to things in the past you can't change. People change, all you can do is move forward. The girls also forgave him and have been chatting and visiting with him since Jess's funeral. I'm glad that the grandchildren will have a grandparent when my time is done.

2 Days Ago

Chapter Sixty

I sat in my chair, staring out the window. Judge Judy reruns were on, but I couldn't focus. Every car that went by made me want to run—well, maybe not run—to the door. Soon, Jordan and Sandy would be here with Julie, John, and my three grandbabies. One of those grandbabies will have my great grandbaby. Jordan rented a van for the week to cart everyone around.

Jordan's car turned into the driveway, driven by Sandy. There was a blonde in giant sunglasses on the passenger side. My heart skipped a beat. *Julie.* A large white van was parked in front of the house. Wiggly William and Smiley Scott jumped out first. Gentle Johnny and Emily followed, with little Softie Sophia in her car seat.

My shaking legs threatened to betray me at any moment, but I stood with my walker as everyone filed in. The beautiful chaos of hellos and hugs ensued.

"I'll put our stuff in our room," John called to Julie over the noise. She blew him a kiss in thanks.

The day before, Jordan set up two air mattresses in the bigger of the two bedrooms for Julie's youngest boys. He also set up one in the other bedroom because Sweet Skye would be in there sleeping with Jen and Shar when they arrived the next day. Gentle Jonny and Emily would sleep in the smallest room with the baby.

Julie turned to me. "Come sit down Ma. I love your hair. Did you go get it done?"

"Thanks, sort of. I didn't go anywhere. Nancy came over this morning and gave me a trim and style. It is pretty great having a hairdresser as a best friend," I answered, touching my curled-under ends.

I held out my hands for Softie Sofia. Emily handed me the three-month-old wonder. Fine blond hair, curious eyes, and hands that waved out to catch anything they could. I inhaled the top of her head for the wonderful aroma combination of milk and diapers babies have.

At dinner, the chaos calmed down and everyone was about to sit down for the hamburgers that Julie and Gentle Johnny cooked. My burger was thinner than the others and had tomatoes and lettuce Sandy brought from the farmer's market in Pawtucket, where they live. My baked potatoes had olive oil instead of butter, and no salt for anything, but I'm used to that.

John rose and prayed before we ate. As I sat there with my head down and my eyes closed, I was convicted about forgetting God in my life. When I wasn't able to get out to church, it was only a matter of time before it was out of sight, out of mind. My Bible got left on the filing cabinet one day and forgotten about, much as I felt I had been forgotten.

Quitting work at sixty, giving up my license at sixty-two, and now at sixty-six years old, no one from work or church has come over in a long time. The only ones who still care to call and visit often are Nancy and my family.

I made a formal apology right there to God in prayer and thanked him for always being here, whether or not I remembered. I said amen with everyone and dug into my potato.

When dessert was over, we were entering the living room when Jen and her crew burst through the door. "Have no fear, we're here. Let the party begin!" Jen shouted, walking in with Rosco on his leash. The boys fawned all over him. He's a three-year-old basset hound and has the longest ears they had ever seen.

Sweet Skye, so tall and grown up, followed her. At twenty-six she's a beauty with her dad's curls and green eyes and her mom's freckles. She hadn't been to visit since she got her job at a design firm in Chicago.

Behind her was Shar, carrying the littlest squishy baby I'd seen in a long time. She gave birth barely one month ago to my youngest grandchild, Timothy, whom I quickly named Twilight Tim.

After kisses and one-armed hugs, Shar set Twilight Tim in my arms. His dark hair and almond eyes are reflections of hers. Asleep, he didn't even budge when he came to rest in my arms. "Wow, a good sleeper. I made a good choice with the nickname 'Twilight.'" I looked over to Jen and Skye, who were filming me with their phones.

"He's a champ," Jen said. "He has already slept through the night twice." She held up two fingers.

"Except for this morning," Sweet Skye put in with an eye roll.

"Oh yes, that's why we're early," Shar said, coming over and touching Twilight's head. "He woke all of us up at four. We decided to pile in the car and start then. There was no traffic for hours. It was great."

I stared down at my tiniest grandson. He stirred and grabbed my hand, bringing it to his mouth.

"No, no, buddy. This is my finger. You need to eat your own fingers," I told him as I disconnected his tiny digits and helped him get his own fingers to his mouth. Watching him jam his hand in his mouth, sucking and slobbering, tears began welling in my eyes and dropped on his little chubby arms.

"Are you okay, Ma?" Julie asked and everyone looked.

"Yes. I'm just amazed at these little ones."

I really *am* amazed by them. Babies' lives are a great joy. They are so full of potential. But my tears were selfish ones. They were tears of not being able to see any of my grandchildren's next birthdays.

Yesterday

Chapter Sixty-One

I woke to sounds I hadn't heard in years, and it took a second to remember that it wasn't 1986 with my girls getting breakfast and heading into the living room for Saturday morning cartoons. Pulling on my housecoat, I checked my reflection to tame a few stray strands. I walk out into a flurry of "Where's my towel?" and "Are those sandwiches ready yet?"

"Oh, morning Ma." Jen kissed me on the cheek as she scooted by me and grabbed three bottles of sunscreen off the washer. "I'm going to Six Flags, but Shar decided to stay home with the baby. Is that okay? Skye too. She'll stay and take care of Rosco."

"How could I say no to that?" I said with a grand smile. Sweet Skye came to my side. She is a head taller than me, so her shoulders are level with my eyes. "I'm pretty boring, you know."

"No way. You do all the things I love. You watch television, eat, and take naps, and with Mr. Roscoe Roo, it will be the perfect day."

My arm went around her waist and my head to her shoulder. "You're great, Sweet."

"Awe, Nana, I love that you still call me that."

"Well, I always have. Why would I stop now, just because you are grown with a job? No way, that's your name," I said, and she kissed my head, then went to help Jen get things into the van.

They all left in a whirlwind of everyone calling goodbye.

For lunch, Shar made us a chicken vegetable medley that was so delicious I couldn't believe it didn't have any salt.

"Nope," she said. "Just chicken, fresh veggies, and olive oil. Oh, and a splash of orange juice."

"Well, it's the best thing I have eaten in months."

"Thanks, Ma. I'm glad you like it."

I've always loved it when people other than my children called me Ma. Growing up, the kid's friends always did too. It feels like I've meant something to them, like I'll leave a piece of myself with them, like I'll be remembered.

Sweet Skye helped me to the deck when it was time for Roscoe to get some exercise. I sat in the porch's shade as she tossed the ball to him.

My mind wandered back to when Luke was trying to convince me the yard was big enough for a dog. He got down and crawled on all fours. He rolled around on the patch of grass as I stood here on the deck with my arms folded. "No way," I said, while laughing at him.

Today was hot. Before long, Rosco and I were both panting to get back to the air-conditioned house. The best thing I ever did to this house was put in central air conditioning.

We all watched television and napped together. Me in my chair, and Shar on the couch with Twilight sleeping on her chest. Sweet was the first to snore on the love seat with Rosco.

At about four-thirty, everyone came piling in with empty coolers, damp towels, and sun-kissed faces.

We ordered pizza. Watching the cheese pull from everyone's mouth and inhaling the sweet red sauce, I was overcome. I decided a half slice of veggie pizza with a little more of the afternoon's chicken and vegetables would be a good dinner.

Savoring the slice, I ate it in small bites, chewing it as long as possible. To my depraved taste buds, it was an explosion of crisp dough, salty cheese, and the ancient delicacy that is tomato sauce. I closed my eyes and let each bite be fully appreciated.

Everyone was alight with the excitement. Passing phones around to see pictures of rides and attractions, I was reminded of all the photos that used to be on the walls from my instant camera.

I don't know if it was the pizza or the chaos, but a panic attack came out of nowhere, with my breath coming in short bursts and my hands shaking. "Jen, can you help me to my chair in the living room?"

"Of course. You okay?" she asked, handing Twilight to Julie.

"Just a little dizzy." She held my arm to help me up. "I just need a little space."

Walking me into the other room, she helped me into my chair. "You sure you don't want to be in your room, or on the porch?"

"No thanks, darlin', I'll be fine here. Go finish your dinner. I wouldn't mind a minute alone." Everyone here was well aware of my claustrophobia.

"I'm surprised you made it this far with everyone in there." She winked at me and handed me the remote. Ever the nurse, she made sure there were no chinks in my oxygen tube.

I expected her to go back into the kitchen and finish her dinner. Instead, she sat on the floor beside me, hugged my legs, and put her head on my lap. "You're a great mother."

It caught me off guard. "Thanks, it takes one to know one."

"I mean it Ma, thank you for always trying to do the best for all of us." I could feel her tears wetting my house coat. I put my hand on her head. She burst into a sob. "I'm sorry," she whispered. "I'm sorry we moved so far. Sorry for not visiting more."

I lifted her head. "Honey, never feel sorry about living your life the way you think you should. You did that to keep your family together. You were making the best choice for Sweet. That is why you are a great mother, too. We do what we must."

"I miss you all the time."

"I miss you too, but this is the way it is supposed to be. Kids leave their parents and make the cycle in their own way. Look at Sweet, she is amazing, and Twilight will be too. Jen, have no regrets about how you have lived. You are amazing and I'm so proud of you."

She set her head back on my lap and we stayed there silently for a minute to recover.

Before long, the others came filtering in.

"Everything okay here?" Gentle asked.

"Yes, just mother-daughter stuff," Jen replied. "You'll see one day." She looked at Emily holding Softie.

The rest of the night was consumed by Harry Potter. Everyone piled on the couches or spread out on the floor, watching Ron ride the knight on the wizard's chess board.

I was drifting in and out and by the end, I was asleep. Julie helped me to bed. She brought the covers up to my chest and kissed my forehead like I used to with her, and she no doubt did with her children. "I love you Ma."

"I love you too," I said, hugging her neck.

"I'm so happy we could be here."

"Me too darlin'. See you in the morning."

"Good night," she said as she almost closed the door. I made a small sound in my throat.

"Oops, don't worry, I won't close it." She left, leaving the door open a crack.

I flicked on the television for light and sound and drifted off to sleep.

Today

Chapter Sixty-Two

Once again, getting up and dressing with the sounds of people next door in the kitchen is disorienting. I could hear the boys telling Sweet about the awesome rides and asking why she didn't go.

"Well," she says. "I wanted to spend time with Nana, and I didn't want Rosco to be lonely."

"Maybe we can go back before we leave," the boys tell her, still not understanding how she could ever want to stay home.

"Maybe," she says as I come out of my room.

"Morning, Ma," Jordan says when he sees me. It was only eight thirty. He and Sandy came over early to spend as much time as possible with everyone. "Is there anything you want to do today?"

"Take lots of pictures," I say on the way to the table. "With a Polaroid like I used to. Do they make those anymore? I'd love to have one of those and have the pictures in my hand today."

"I'll go get one or figure out something similar," Jordan says as he pops up and leaves to search it out.

"While he finds that out, can I get some pictures of you and the boys with my phone?" Sweet asks.

"Only if they'll make silly faces with me." That's all I had to say, and they're next to me in a second. Sticking out their tongues and pushing fingers up to flatten their noses. In most of the pictures, we are cross-eyed.

Just before ten, Jordan comes in with a Polaroid camera and tons of film. The hard plastic was familiar in my hand and the sound of the film sliding into its spot brings back a special feeling of younger days. Pressing the action button, I grab the picture and do the unnecessary development wave as an automatic response.

The afternoon is spent out back on the porch with Sweet. We're taking photos of Jordan and the boys playing with the hose and giving Roscoe a bath. I take shots of all the laughs and screams and dog shakes that my film will allow. After more laughter than I have had in a long time, we come back into the air-conditioned house and look at our stack of photos.

Sandy picked out one in particular. "This one's my favorite." It's one of Jordan and Wiggly soaping up the dog. Rosco is in full shake. Both boys were holding out their hands and turning away to hold back the unstoppable soapy water. "That's hilarious."

John and Julie make potato salad and tuna sandwiches for dinner, per my request. After dinner, we take pictures of me with everyone together and separately.

"A perfect day," I say, settling down in my chair. "Laughing really takes a lot out of you."

"What time does the game start?" Jen asks. She's talking about the Red Sox game. She knows I usually watch everyone I can.

"We don't have to watch that. Let's watch something for the kids."

"We love baseball," Wiggly and Smiley say in unison.

"Well then, it's on now. Probably in the second inning," I say, looking at the clock.

I pop the screen on with the remote and everyone files into the living room. Julie put Softie on my lap. I turn her to see the screen and she starts waving her arms and shouting baby talk taunts at the other team. "She's a baseball fan in training."

"You tell ' 'em Sophie. The Sox got this. You tell 'em," John calls.

John and Julie squish on the couch with Sandy and Jordan. Jen, Shar, and Twilight are on the love seat. Gentle and Emily are on kitchen chairs brought in from the other room, and Rosco and the boys line the floor; all of them on their tummies looking up at the screen. And Sweet Skye is sitting on the floor by my side. A spot she's barely left since she got here.

I stay awake as long as I can, not wanting the day to end. Eventually, I have to give in. Sweet helps me down the hall and to my room. I sit on the bed and pat the spot next to me. She sits with me. "Thank you for today. You are my first grandbaby, Sweet. It was special to have some time sharing an old love of mine that seems to be a love of yours."

"I had a great time, too. Yes, I love photography."

I reach into the basket of my walker. "When you leave, I want you to take the camera. I know it isn't fancy, but maybe you'll use it and think of today and remember me."

"Nana, thank you," she says, taking the camera. "I'll take it, but I won't need it to remember you. I love you. I'll never forget today."

We're both a little teary in our hug, then she gets up to rejoin the others in the living room.

"Love you, Sweet Skye," I call on my way to the bathroom.

"Love you too, Sweet Nana." She smiled as she shut the door.

While I brush my teeth, I start to feel dizzy. Happy to lie down in bed, I pull the covers up and shut my eyes. As I drift off to sleep, I hear the far-off sound of everyone talking. I detect the faintest hint of toast. Wondering who would be snacking this late makes me smile. *I bet it's Sweet Skye*, is my last thought.

Jordan

Epilogue

I'm already awake when the six a.m. call from Skye lights up my phone. As I swipe my screen to answer, I can hear Sandy dealing with the effects of morning sickness in the bathroom. Smiling to myself, I can't wait to tell everyone at breakfast this morning about our bundle expected in early spring.

"Hey Skye, what's up?"

The early summer sun reflects off the hardwood floors and brings an orange glow to the white furniture and quilt of my in-laws' guest room.

"Jordan, I'm sorry to call so early, but it's Nana." My knees lock, bringing me to standing. My fingers and toes are instantly cold and numb.

She continues through sniffled back sobs. "She passed in the night. I found her this morning. Mom and Auntie are a wreck. Can you guys come over soon?"

I've thought of getting this call for years. Still somehow, it's caught me off guard. "Have you called the police or anyone yet?"

"No, Mom said we should have everyone here first." Skye coughs out another sob. "Please come as soon as you can."

"Yes, of course. Right away, let me just tell Sandy." Pressing the end button on the screen, I look up to see Sandy leaning on the doorway for support. Tears in her eyes, she guessed what the call was about.

***

I left Sandy asleep in bed. My body is wracked with exhaustion from the last few days. My puffy, swollen eyes make it hard to focus on the doorway as I amble to the bathroom.

One look in the mirror tells me I'm not ready for this day. In the shower, the warm water wakes my senses, and a small amount of energy trickles back into my body.

Still unstable, I move to the kitchen for coffee. I sit there with my warm cup of dark liquid at the table with my head in my hand. The ringing quiet of my mother-in-law's house presses in all around me. I push my way to standing and finish getting ready.

Here at the funeral home, shaking hands in a row with my siblings is surreal. Some people have come that I have known all my life, and then also people I hardly know. I'm no stranger to funerals, although it has been a while. The cross emotions of hearing "Oh, it's great to see you," and "Sorry for your loss," are hard to work out. Stories about how my mother has touched people's lives and reliving the moments before her death are almost unbearable.

It's time for someone to go up and speak. That someone is me. As I pass the poster titled BETH in big glitter letters, I touch a few of the photos. I step up to the podium, something I'd only do for her, and unfold my notes.

"Most of you know Ma passed quickly and quietly in her sleep. She didn't tell any of us she had asked Dr. Martinez to turn off her implanted defibrillator. Knowing medicine was no longer any help for her condition, she wanted to slip out peacefully when the time came. We were all visiting last week, and she was full of love when she went to bed on Friday night. No one would have guessed that it would be an aneurysm that would end her life," I said and took a breath.

"Anyone who has ever known me knows how much I loved my mother. She was a rock for all her kids and anyone else who needed help. Some of you know her as Beth, but most of you know her simply as Ma. She offered her time and her love from an immeasurable well. She was unsinkable for sixty-six years; through childhood trauma, abuse, heart attacks, cancer, surgeries, not to mention the loss of her husband and daughter." My eyes close a moment to get hold of the harsh reminder both my parents are gone, and I'm only thirty.

"She was never as happy or as proud as when she was holding a newborn baby. Whether it was her child, grandchild, or her great grandchild. As the youngest of my siblings, I was in a very privileged position to talk with her and listen to her reflect on her mistakes and her memories, her regrets, and her understanding that you can't change what was, no matter how much you want to, you just have to do what you can now. Despite her missteps and flaws, she was a mother through and through, and she loved all her kids more than anything," I said, making air quotes on kids. "She was a shoulder to cry on or an ear to listen to everyone in her life. She thought of all our friends as her kids.

"It's the single most important thing I've taken with me through life, and she gave that to me. Love is free. Give as much of it as often as you can. Now we will bring her to her final resting place, but she will stay with all of us in every fiber of our being forever."

The funeral director, seeing that I'm done with my eulogy, but can't quite move, comes up to the podium and said, "Thank you, Jordan, that was lovely." I leave the podium, and he says a few closing words about where the people are to go next.

After a group hug with Sandy, Julie, and Jen, we all are full of tears, with some spilling out. The rest of the day and the rest of my life is filled with memories of my mother and the lessons she taught me.

Acknowledgments

This book would not have been possible without the exceptional people God brought into my life at just the right time. First, I want to thank my husband and son for their love, support, and encouragement. Next, to my early readers, thank you for your helpful insight and keen eyes. Also, many thanks to my editor Kristin McTiernan at The Nonsense-Free Editor, and Suzanne McCaig at Inknot Publishing. Finally, a special thanks to all the women I know who shared stories of their lives in the 1950s, 60s, and 70s.

About the Author

I live in northern New England. I'm a freelance copy editor and proofreader when I'm not writing. If I have a minute when I'm not writing or editing, I love to walk my dog and bake bread.

Please feel free to follow me on Facebook and Instagram @rosmarytoppiauthor

If you enjoyed my book, please take a moment to leave a review. It's the best thank you I could get.